The Book of Animal Stories

The Book of Animal Stories

Edited by Lesley O'Mara

MICHAEL O'MARA BOOKS LIMITED

To J.J.

First published in Great Britain 1989 by
Michael O'Mara Books Limited
20 Queen Anne Street
London W1N 9FB

British Library Cataloguing in Publication Data

The book of animal stories
  1. Children's short stories in English.
  Special subjects: Animal – Anthologies
  I. O'Mara, Lesley
  823.'01'0836 [J]

Design: Mick Keates

Typeset by Florencetype, Kewstoke, Avon
Printed and bound in Great Britain
by Mackays of Chatham PLC

Contents

Brer Rabbit

from *Tales of Uncle Remus*
Traditional

1) HOW THE ANIMALS CAME TO EARTH

THIS may come as a surprise to you, but the animals haven't always lived on earth. Long, long ago, they lived beside the moon, and would probably still be there if Brer Rabbit hadn't had a big quarrel with Sister Moon. This is what happened:

The animals used to sit in their gardens on fine evenings, and they liked looking at Sister Moon because they thought that she was so beautiful. But they noticed that she was getting thinner. In fact she looked so skinny that you would have thought she had gone on a strict diet.

Brer Rabbit made up his mind to find out what was the matter with her. He climbed over the fence and spoke to her. 'Are you alright, Sister Moon? You don't look like your usual self to me.'

Sister Moon replied, 'I haven't been feeling too well lately.'

'Can I do anything to help you?'

'Thanks all the same, Brer Rabbit, but I don't think

you are the man who can do what I need to be done.'
That annoyed Brer Rabbit. 'I can do better than Brer
Sun who you chase over the sky every month but never
manage to catch.'

This made Sister Moon smile – 'Very well, Brer
Rabbit, I will let you try. I want to let Mr Man know that
I seem to have got a cold through being out in the night
air so much. I need to put out my light for a while and
have a little holiday before I get any worse. I don't want
Mr Man to look up one night and be afraid when he sees
there is no light.'

'Don't worry, Sister Moon. I'll take him your message.
I have been wanting to see what Mr Man looks like any
how.'

Brer Rabbit repeated what he had to say then away he
went.

He ran very fast then took a long, long jump. He
tumbled head over heels through space, down past the
stars and through the galaxy, feeling more and more
scared as he went. In fact he was so scared that his eyes
got bigger and bigger and nearly popped right out of his
head. They have stayed like that to this very day.

At last he landed on Earth, and checked to make sure
that he was still all in one piece. When he found that he
was still all there, he looked around him. The first thing
he saw was Mr Man's vegetable garden, filled with green
peas, lettuce, cabbage, carrots and sparrow grass. Brer
Rabbit's mouth started watering. In a field nearby he
saw sheep, cows, goats and pigs.

He went and knocked on the door of Mr Man's house
and said, 'I have brought you a message from Sister
Moon.'

'What is it?'

Brer Rabbit had to think for a minute.

'She said "I am getting weak so I am going to where
the shadows stay." '

Mr Man got cross. 'Tell Sister Moon I said that if we

don't see her we'll soon forget her, and when she is dead her feet will get cold.'

Brer Rabbit nodded and jumped right up again back to Sister Moon. When he told her what Mr Man had said she got angry. She took hold of a shovel and swiped him across the face so hard that she split his lip. Brer Rabbit wasn't standing for that. So he clawed and scratched her right back. You can still see the marks on both of them – rabbits have split lips and the face of the moon has scratches and holes in it.

Brer Rabbit went and told the animals what he had seen on Earth – the vegetables, cows, sheep, goats and fat pigs. They all decided that they would leave Sister Moon by herself from then on. So they all took that long, long jump and they have been here on Earth ever since.

2) HOW BRER FOX AND BRER RABBIT BECAME ENEMIES

After the animals started living on Earth, things started to change amongst them. Instead of being friends with each other, as they used to be, they started to argue and quarrel. In fact, in a short time they became as quarrelsome as people.

One day Brer Fox and Brer Rabbit were sitting together by the road chatting about nothing in particular when they heard a strange noise – biff, biff, biff.

'What's that?,' asked Brer Fox. He was wondering if it was anything to be scared of.

'That?' answered Brer Rabbit, 'It sounds to me like Sister Goose.'

'What is she doing?'

'Biffing clothes,' said Brer Rabbit.

You won't understand what that means these days. Now you take your dirty clothes to a laundrette, or you have a washing machine and a dryer in your own house.

Long ago there were no such things, and people used to take their dirty washing to a stream or river. They got their clothes really wet, then beat the dirt out of them with a biffing stick. It really made things as clean as new snow.

Well, as soon as Brer Fox knew that Sister Goose was down at the stream, his greedy eyes got big and Brer Rabbit knew that he was thinking about his supper. Brer Fox said that he had better be going home, and Brer Rabbit said that he should do the same, so they each went their own way. But Brer Rabbit doubled back and went down to the stream where Sister Goose was busy.

'How are you today, Sister Goose?'

'I'm fine, thank you, Brer Rabbit. I am sorry I can't shake hands with you, but they are all full of suds.' Brer Rabbit said he quite understood.

Now you must be thinking that a goose doesn't have hands. Well, that's true enough, but she has to use what she has got to take the place of hands.

After Brer Rabbit and Sister Goose had finished passing the time of day, Brer Rabbit said, 'I want to warn you about Brer Fox. He is coming to get you, Sister Goose, and it will probably be before tomorrow morning.'

Sister Goose was really scared to hear that.

'What can I do, Brer Rabbit? My husband is dead, and there is no man about the house. What am I going to do?'

Brer Rabbit thought for a while.

'Roll all your clothes inside a clean white sheet, and put that in your bed tonight. Then you go and sleep in the rafters.'

So Sister Goose agreed to do that, but she also sent for her friend Brer Dog. She asked him if he would keep watch for the night, and he said that he would be glad to do that.

Just before it was light, Brer Fox crept up to the house, gently pushed open the door and slipped inside. He saw something big and white on the bed, so he grabbed it and ran out of the door. Just as he jumped off the porch, Brer Dog came out from under the house growling in a menacing way. Brer Fox dropped the bundle of clothes as if it was on fire, and dashed away just as fast as he could go.

It was a good thing for Brer Dog too, because it had taken him four months to find anyone able to wash and iron his pyjamas as well as Sister Goose, so he didn't want anything to happen to her.

The next day the news got around that Brer Fox had tried to steal Sister Goose's laundry and he was afraid to show his face for a week. Brer Fox blamed Brer Dog for spreading the story around, and ever since then the dog and the fox haven't been friends.

3) HOLD HIM DOWN, BRER FOX

Brer Fox got to know that it was Brer Rabbit who had warned Sister Goose that he was coming to get her, and he made up his mind that he would get his own back. Brer Rabbit also got to know what was in Brer Fox's mind, so he stayed away from his usual haunts for a while.

One day, however, he was roaming around when he saw a big horse lying in a pasture as if he were dead. The horse's tail twitched, though, so he knew that he just looked that way. Brer Rabbit kept on going, when who should he meet but Brer Fox!

'Brer Fox, Brer Fox. Come and see. Come here quickly. I have some good news for you.'

Brer Fox wasn't interested in what good news Brer Rabbit had. The best news for him was that he had found Brer Rabbit. But before Brer Fox could grab him,

Brer Rabbit said, 'Come on, Brer Fox. I have found something to give us fresh meat until next September.'

Brer Fox was always a cautious fellow, but he wanted to know more. 'What are you talking about, Brer Rabbit?'

'I have just found a horse lying on the ground where we can catch him and tie him up.'

Brer Fox liked the sound of that so he said, 'O.K. Let's go.'

Brer Rabbit led him to the pasture, and true to his word there was the horse lying on the ground just as if he was waiting for them.

Brer Rabbit and Brer Fox started talking about the best way to tie him up. They argued this way and that way until at last Brer Rabbit said, 'Listen, I have thought of the best way to do it. I'll tie him to your tail then you can hold him down when he tries to get up. I would do it myself if I were big and strong like you but I am too weak and I wouldn't be able to hold him. Of course if you are scared to do it we'll have to think of another way.'

There was something about this plan which seemed wrong to Brer Fox but he couldn't think what it was. He wanted Brer Rabbit to think that he was brave and strong so he agreed with the plan.

Brer Rabbit tied him to the horse's tail. 'Brer Fox, now that horse is really caught, though he doesn't know it.' Brer Fox gave a sickly grin. Brer Rabbit got a great long branch and hit the horse on the rump – BANG! The horse jumped up onto his feet and Brer Fox was left hanging onto his tail, upside down and too far off the ground for his liking.

'Hold 'im down, Brer Fox! Hold 'im down!'

The horse snorted and jumped and bucked and twirled, but still Brer Fox held on.

'Hold 'im down, Brer Fox! Hold 'im down!'

Once Brer Fox shouted back, 'If I got him down,

who'd get hold of me?'

But Brer Rabbit kept on yelling the same thing over and over.

The horse kicked with his hind legs, and at last Brer Fox managed to slide down his tail. The horse kicked him in the stomach three times and Brer Fox went flying through the air.

It was a week and four days before Brer Fox came down to earth, and that gave him plenty of time to realise that Brer Rabbit had got the better of him again.

The Ugly Duckling

by Hans Christian Andersen

IT was beautiful in the country, it was summer-time; the wheat was yellow, the oats were green, the hay was stacked up in the green meadows, and the stork paraded about on his long red legs, discoursing in Egyptian, which language he had learned from his mother. The fields and meadows were skirted by thick woods, and a deep lake lay in the midst of the woods. – Yes, it was indeed beautiful in the country! The sunshine fell warmly on an old mansion, surrounded by deep canals, and from the walls down to the water's edge there grew large burdock-leaves, so high that children could stand upright among them without being perceived. This place was as wild and unfrequented as the thickest part of the woods, and on that account a duck had chosen to make her nest there. She was sitting on her eggs; but the pleasure she had felt at first was now almost gone, because she had been there so long, and had so few visitors, for the other ducks preferred swimming on the canals to sitting among the burdock-leaves gossiping with her.

At last the eggs cracked one after another, 'Tchick, tchick!' All the eggs were alive, and one little head after another appeared. 'Quack, quack,' said the duck, and all got up as well as they could; they peeped about from under the green leaves, and as green is good for the eyes, their mother let them look as long as they pleased.

'How large the world is!' said the little ones, for they found their present situation very different to their former confined one, while yet in the egg-shells.

'Do you imagine this to be the whole of the world?' said the mother; 'it extends far beyond the other side of the garden, to the pastor's field; but I have never been there. Are you all here?' And then she got up. 'No, I have not got you all, the largest egg is still here. How long will this last? I am so weary of it!' And then she sat down again.

'Well, and how are you getting on?' asked an old duck, who had come to pay her a visit.

'This one egg keeps me so long,' said the mother, 'it will not break. But you should see the others; they are the prettiest little ducklings I have seen in all my days; they are all like their father – the good-for-nothing fellow! he has not been to visit me once.'

'Let me see the egg that will not break,' said the old duck; 'depend upon it, it is a turkey's egg. I was cheated in the same way once myself, and I had such trouble with the young ones; for they were afraid of the water, and I could not get them there. I called and scolded, but it was all of no use. But let me see the egg – ah yes! to be sure, that is a turkey's egg. Leave it and teach the other little ones to swim.'

'I will sit on it a little longer,' said the duck. 'I have been sitting so long, that I may as well spend the harvest here.'

'It is no business of mine,' said the old duck, and away she waddled.

The great egg burst at last, 'Tchick, tchick,' said the

little one, and out it tumbled – but oh, how large and ugly it was! The duck looked at it. 'That is a great, strong creature,' she said; 'none of the the others are at all like it; can it be a young turkey-cock? Well, we shall soon find out; it must go into the water, though I push it in myself!'

The next day there was delightful weather, and the sun shone warmly upon all the green leaves when mother-duck with all her family went down to the canal; plump she went into the water, 'Quack, quack,' cried she, and one duckling after another jumped in. The water closed over their heads, but all came up again, and swam together in the pleasantest manner; their legs moved without effort. All were there, even the ugly grey one.

'No! it is not a turkey,' said the old duck; 'only see how prettily it moves its legs, how upright it holds itself; it is my own child! it is also really very pretty when one looks more closely at it; quack, quack, now come with me, I will take you into the world, introduce you in the duck-yard; but keep close to me, or someone may tread on you, and beware of the cat.'

So they came into the duck-yard. There was a horrid noise; two families were quarrelling about the remains of an eel, which in the end was secured by the cat.

'See, my children, such is the way of the world,' said the mother-duck, wiping her beak, for she too was fond of roasted eels. 'Now use your legs,' she said, 'keep together, and bow to the old duck you see yonder. She is the most distinguished of all the fowls present, and is of Spanish blood, which accounts for her dignified appearance and manners. And look, she has a red rag on her leg; that is considered extremely handsome, and is the greatest distinction a duck can have. Don't turn your feet inwards; a well-educated duckling always keeps his legs apart, like his father and mother, just so – look, now bow your necks, and say "quack." '

And they did as they were told. But the other ducks who were in the yard looked at them and said aloud, 'Only see, now we have another brood, as if there were not enough of us already. And fie! how ugly that one is! We will not endure it'; and immediately one of the ducks flew at him, and bit him in the neck.

'Leave him alone,' said the mother, 'he is doing no one any harm.'

'Yes, but he is so large, and so strange-looking, and therefore he shall be teased.'

'Those are fine children that our good mother has,' said the old duck with the red rag on her leg. 'All are pretty except one, and that has not turned out well; I almost wish it could be hatched over again.'

'That cannot be, please your highness,' said the mother. 'Certainly he is not handsome, but he is a very good child, and swims as well as the others, indeed rather better. I think he will grow like the others all in good time, and perhaps will look smaller. He stayed so long in the egg-shell, that is the cause of the difference,' and she scratched the duckling's neck, and stroked his whole body. 'Besides,' added she, 'he is a drake; I think he will be very strong, therefore it does not matter so much; he will fight his way through.'

'The other ducks are very pretty,' said the old duck, 'pray make yourselves at home, and if you find an eel's head you can bring it to me.'

And accordingly they made themselves at home.

But the poor little duckling, who had come last out of its egg-shell, and who was so ugly, was bitten, pecked, and teased by both ducks and hens. 'It is so large,' said they all. And the turkey-cock, who had come into the world with spurs on, and therefore fancied he was an emperor, puffed himself up like a ship in full sail, and marched up to the duckling quite red with passion. The poor little thing scarcely knew what to do; he was quite distressed because he was so ugly, and because he was the jest of the poultry-yard.

So passed the first day, and afterwards matters grew worse and worse; the poor duckling was scorned by all. Even his brothers and sisters behaved unkindly, and were constantly saying, 'The cat fetch thee, thou nasty creature!' The mother said, 'Ah, if thou wert only far away!' The ducks bit him, the hens pecked him, and the girl who fed the poultry kicked him. He ran over the hedge; the little birds in the bushes were terrified. 'That is because I am so ugly,' thought the duckling, shutting his eyes, but he ran on. At last he came to a wide moor, where lived some wild ducks; here he lay the whole night, so tired and so comfortless. In the morning the wild ducks flew up, and perceived their new companion. 'Pray, who are you?' asked they; and our little duckling turned himself in all directions, and greeted them as politely as possible.

'You are really uncommonly ugly,' said the wild ducks; 'however, that does not matter to us, provided you do not marry into our families.' Poor thing! he had never thought of marrying; he only begged permission to lie among the reeds, and drink the water of the moor.

There he lay for two whole days – on the third day there came two wild geese, or rather ganders, who had not been long out of their egg-shells, which accounts for their impertinence.

'Hark ye,' said they, 'you are so ugly that we like you infinitely well; will you come with us, and be a bird of passage? On another moor, not far from this, are some dear, sweet, wild geese, as lovely creatures as have ever said "hiss, hiss." You are truly in the way to make your fortune, ugly as you are.'

Bang! a gun went off all at once, and both wild geese were stretched dead among the reeds; the water became red with blood – bang! a gun went off again, whole flocks of wild geese flew up from among the reeds, and another report followed.

There was a grand hunting party: the hunters lay in ambush all around; some were even sitting in the trees, whose huge branches stretched far over the moor. The blue smoke rose through the thick trees like a mist, and was dispersed as it fell over the water; the hounds splashed about in the mud, the reeds and rushes bent in all directions. How frightened the poor little duck was! He turned his head, thinking to hide it under his wings, and in a moment a most formidable-looking dog stood close to him, his tongue hanging out of his mouth, his eyes sparkling fearfully. He opened his wide jaws at the sight of our duckling, showed him his sharp teeth, and, splash, splash! he was gone, gone without hurting him.

'Well! let me be thankful,' sighed he, 'I am so ugly, that even the dog will not eat me.'

And now he lay still, though the shooting continued among the reeds, shot following shot.

The noise did not cease till late in the day, and even then the poor little thing dared not stir; he waited several hours before he looked around him, and then hastened away from the moor as fast as he could. He ran over fields and meadows, though the wind was so high that he had some difficulty in proceeding.

Towards evening he reached a wretched little hut, so wretched that it knew not on which side to fall, and therefore remained standing. The wind blew violently, so that our poor little duckling was obliged to support himself on his tail, in order to stand against it; but it became worse and worse. He then remarked that the door had lost one of its hinges, and hung so much awry that he could creep through the crevice into the room, which he did.

In this room lived an old woman, with her tom-cat and her hen; and the cat, whom she called her little son, knew how to set up his back and purr; indeed, he could even emit sparks when stroked the wrong way. The hen had very short legs, and was therefore called 'Cuckoo

Shortlegs'; she laid very good eggs, and the old woman loved her as her own child.

The next morning the new guest was perceived; the cat began to mew, and the hen to cackle.

'What is the matter?' asked the old woman, looking round; however, her eyes were not good, so she took the young duckling to be a fat duck who had lost her way. 'This is a capital catch,' said she, 'I shall now have duck's eggs, if it be not a drake: we must try.'

And so the duckling was put to the proof for three weeks, but no eggs made their appearance.

Now the cat was the master of the house, and the hen was the mistress, and they used always to say, 'We and the World,' for they imagined themselves to be not only the half of the world, but also by far the better half. The duckling thought it was possible to be of a different opinion, but that the hen would not allow.

'Can you lay eggs?' asked she.

'No.'

'Well, then, hold your tongue.'

And the cat said, 'Can you set up your back? can you purr?'

'No.'

'Well, then, you should have no opinion when reasonable persons are speaking.'

So the duckling sat alone in a corner, and was in a very bad humour; however, he happened to think of the fresh air and bright sunshine, and these thoughts gave him such a strong desire to swim again that he could not help telling it to the hen.

'What ails you?' said the hen. 'You have nothing to do, and, therefore, brood over these fancies; either lay eggs, or purr, then you will forget them.'

'But it is so delicious to swim,' said the duckling, 'so delicious when the waters close over your head, and you plunge to the bottom.'

'Well, that is a queer sort of a pleasure,' said the hen;

And the cat said, 'Can you purr?'

'I think you must be crazy. Not to speak of myself, ask the cat – he is the most sensible animal I know – whether he would like to swim or to plunge to the bottom of the water. Ask our mistress, the old woman – there is no one in the world wiser than she – do you think she would take pleasure in swimming, and in the waters closing over her head?'

'You do not understand me,' said the duckling.

'What, we do not understand you! so you think yourself wiser than the cat, and the old woman, not to speak of myself. Do not fancy any such thing, child, but be thankful for all the kindness that has been shown you. Are you not lodged in a warm room, and have you not the advantage of society from which you can learn something? But you are a simpleton, and it is wearisome to have anything to do with you. Believe me, I wish you well. I tell you unpleasant truths, but it is thus that real friendship is shown. Come, for once give yourself the trouble to learn to purr, or to lay eggs.'

'I think I will go out into the wide world again,' said the duckling.

'Well, go,' answered the hen.

So the duckling went. He swam on the surface of the water, he plunged beneath, but all animals passed him by, on account of his ugliness. And the autumn came, the leaves turned yellow and brown, the wind caught them and danced them about, the air was very cold, the clouds were heavy with hail or snow, and the raven sat on the hedge and croaked: – the poor duckling was certainly not very comfortable!

One evening, just as the sun was setting with unusual brilliancy, a flock of large beautiful birds rose from out of the brushwood; the duckling had never seen anything so beautiful before; their plumage was of a dazzling white and they had long, slender necks. They were swans; they uttered a singular cry, spread out their long, splendid wings, and flew away from these cold regions to warmer countries, across the open sea. They flew so high, so very high! and the little ugly duckling's feelings were so strange; he turned round and round in the water like a mill-wheel, strained his neck to look after them, and sent forth such a loud and strange cry, that it almost frightened himself. – Ah! he could not forget them, those noble birds! those happy birds! When he could see them no longer, he plunged to the bottom of the water, and when he rose again was almost beside himself. The duckling knew not what the birds were called, knew not whither they were flying, yet he loved them as he had never before loved anything; he envied them not, it would never have occurred to him to wish such beauty for himself; he would have been quite contented if the duck in the duck-yard had but endured his company – the poor ugly animal!

And the winter was so cold, so cold! The duckling was obliged to swim round and round in the water, to keep it from freezing; but every night the opening in which he swam became smaller and smaller; it froze so that the crust of ice crackled; the duckling was obliged to make good use of his legs to prevent the water from freezing entirely; at last, wearied out, he lay stiff and cold in the ice.

Early in the morning there passed by a peasant, who saw him, broke the ice in pieces with his wooden shoe, and brought him home to his wife.

He now revived; the children would have played with him, but our duckling thought they wished to tease him, and in his terror jumped into the milk-pail, so that the milk was spilled about the room: the good woman screamed and clapped her hands; he flew thence into the pan where the butter was kept, and thence into the meal-barrel, and out again, and then how strange he looked!

The woman screamed, and struck at him with the tongs; the children ran races with each other trying to

And everyone said, 'The new one is the best'

catch him, and laughed and screamed likewise. It was well for him that the door stood open; he jumped out among the bushes into the new-fallen snow – he lay there as in a dream.

But it would be too melancholy to relate all the trouble and misery that he was obliged to suffer during the severity of the winter – he was lying on a moor among the reeds, when the sun began to shine warmly again, the larks sang, and beautiful spring had returned.

And once more he shook his wings. They were stronger than formerly, and bore him forwards quickly, and before he was well aware of it, he was in a large garden where the apple-trees stood in full bloom, where the syringas sent forth their fragrance and hung their long green branches down into the winding canal. Oh, everything was so lovely, so full of the freshness of spring!

And out of the thicket came three beautiful white swans. They displayed their feathers so proudly, and swam so lightly, so lightly! The duckling knew the glorious creatures, and was seized with a strange melancholy.

'I will fly to them, those kingly birds!' said he. 'They will kill me, because I, ugly as I am, have presumed to approach them; but it matters not, better to be killed by them than to be bitten by the ducks, pecked by the hens, kicked by the girl who feeds the poultry, and to have so much to suffer during the winter!' He flew into the water, and swam towards the beautiful creatures – they saw him and shot forward to meet him. 'Only kill me,' said the poor animal, and he bowed his head low, expecting death – but what did he see in the water? – he saw beneath him his own form, no longer that of a plump, ugly, grey bird – it was that of a swan.

It matters not to have been born in a duck-yard, if one has been hatched from a swan's egg.

The good creature felt himself really elevated by all the troubles and adversities he had experienced. He could now rightly estimate his own happiness, and the larger swans swam round him, and stroked him with their beaks. Some little children were running about in the garden; they threw grain and bread into the water, and the youngest exclaimed, 'There is a new one!' – the others also cried out, 'Yes, there is a new swan come!' and they clapped their hands, and danced around. They ran to their father and mother, bread and cake were thrown into the water and everyone said, 'The new one is the best, so young, and so beautiful!' and the old swans bowed before him. The young swan felt quite ashamed, and hid his head under his wings; he scarcely knew what to do, he was all too happy, but still not proud, for a good heart is never proud. He remembered how he had been persecuted and derided, and he now heard everyone say he was the most beautiful of all beautiful birds. The syringas bent down their branches towards him low into the water, and the sun shone so warmly and brightly – he shook his feathers, stretched his slender neck, and in the joy of his heart said, 'How little did I dream of so much happiness when I was the ugly, despised duckling!'

The Magpie's Lesson

by Muriel Holland

WHEN the birds first began to build nests, long, long ago, it was only the magpie (so they say) who knew how to build one properly.

The other birds tried very hard, but all they could do was to make an untidy pile of sticks or feathers – but they could make nothing that really looked like a nest.

They watched the magpie, with her long tail and beautiful black and white feathers, flying about collecting materials, and making her nest; but whatever they did, they could never build one like hers.

At last, they decided to go to her and ask if she would be kind enough to give them a lesson, and teach them the proper way to build a nest.

The magpie was very pleased with herself, and proud that she was the only one who knew the way to make a nest, so when they came and asked her, she said: 'Yes, certainly I will show you – but you must collect the materials yourselves.'

The birds said they would be glad to do that.

'Well, these are the things I shall want,' said the

magpie. 'First of all, some sticks.'

'I'll collect those,' croaked the crow.

'And, of course, some moss,' continued the magpie.

'I'll get the moss,' piped up the wren.

'Good!' said the magpie, 'then I must have a few feathers.'

'I'll bring the feathers,' twittered the sparrow.

'And I'd like a few pieces of straw.'

'I'd like to get the straw,' cried the starling.

'And some mud,' went on the magpie.

'I'll fetch the mud. I'll fetch the mud,' said the thrush, repeating himself, as usual.

'Also, a few bits of grass.'

'I'll get those,' said the jackdaw, 'Nothing easier.'

'And perhaps a few pieces of wool,' ended the magpie.

'Leave that to me!' called the blackbird, in a loud and important voice. 'I'll get a few pieces of wool for you.'

So it was arranged, and the birds were to meet the magpie again in two days' time. After two days, the birds all gathered together, and the magpie started to give them a lesson.

'First of all,' she said, 'you must lay two sticks across, like this,' and she picked up two sticks, and laid them across each other.

'Aye,' said the crow, 'I thought that was the way to begin.'

'Next,' said the magpie, picking up a feather, 'you add a feather, so!'

'I knew you'd be putting a feather next,' said the jackdaw.

The magpie said nothing, but picked up a piece of moss.

'And now,' she said, 'you add a piece of moss, like this, pressing it gently on top of the feather.'

'Well, of course!' cried the starling, 'anyone could have told you to use a piece of moss next.'

'And now you add a piece of grass,' went on the

magpie, still taking no notice of the interruptions.

'I felt sure you would use a piece of grass next,' piped up the wren.

'Then, after you've done that,' continued the magpie, 'you take up another stick, and place it beside the moss, just as you see me doing.'

'Well, no one can say that is difficult,' said the sparrow, 'I could have done that with no one to teach me at all. Just put a stick beside a piece of moss! Good gracious! There's nothing in that. It's perfectly simple!'

The magpie flew over to the spot where all the materials were gathered together, and picked up a piece of mud in her beak. Then she flew back to the nest, and presented it neatly upon the moss.

'Now, you see what I've done,' she said, 'pressed some mud on top of the moss. That, my friends, is the next thing to do.'

'Well!' cried the tit, 'I could do that standing on my head! It's the easiest thing in the world – just take a little mud, and press it on top of the moss. Fancy bothering to have a lesson to do that. I could do it,' he repeated, 'on my head.'

Still the magpie didn't make any remark, but just went on with her lesson.

'Now, if you take a piece of straw, as I do now, and push it gently between this stick and that piece of moss – so! – you see it helps to keep the whole thing together – '

'Ha! Ha! Ha!' laughed the woodpecker, 'a piece of straw between the stick and the moss. How very simple!'

'And now again,' said the magpie, at last beginning to lose patience, 'another stick, so!' and she banged down another stick on top of the half-built nest.

'Another stick!' exclaimed the thrush, 'another stick! Fancy us all collected here, just to be told "another stick." Why that is something I could have told you almost before I came out of the egg,' and he started to laugh, and the blackbird joined in, and then the starling, and then the sparrow, until soon all the birds were laughing, and repeating after the thrush: 'Another stick!'

This was too much for the magpie, who, after all, had been doing her best to help them. 'Silence!' she cried in a harsh and angry voice, and all the birds were suddenly quite quiet.

'My friends!' said the magpie, 'you make it very clear to me that you all know perfectly well how to build a nest, so it is waste of time my telling you any more about it. I will say nothing of your manners,' she added, 'I will only wish you – Good Day!' And she angrily shook out her wings, and flew swiftly away from them.

The birds looked at each other, rather surprised.

'She has only shown us how to build half a nest,' said the blackbird.

'Perfectly true,' added the thrush.

'I don't call that much of a lesson, when you're only taught half a thing,' said the sparrow.

The pigeon hadn't said anything all along. 'Considering how you all behaved,' she now said very quietly, 'I think we are lucky to have been taught to build even half a nest, and for my part, I am going to start practising at once.' Then she flew away into the wood, leaving the other birds still chattering together.

So that is how it is that, even to-day, most birds still only know how to build half a nest, and they don't add a top to their nest like the magpie does.

Prince Rabbit

by A.A. Milne

ONCE upon a time there was a king who had no children. Sometimes he would say to the queen, 'If only we had a son!' and the queen would answer, 'If only we had!' Another day he would say, 'If only we had a daughter!' and the queen would sigh and answer, 'Yes, even if we had a daughter, that would be something.' But they had no children at all.

As the years went on, and there were still no children in the royal palace, the people began to ask each other who would be the next king to reign over them. And some said that perhaps it would be the chancellor, which was a pity, as nobody liked him very much; and others said that there would be no king at all, but that everybody would be equal. Those who were lowest of all thought that this would be a satisfactory ending of the matter, but those who were higher up felt that, though in some respects it would be a good thing, yet in other respects it would be an ill-advised state of affairs; and they hoped, therefore, that a young prince would be born in the palace. But no prince was born.

One day, when the chancellor was in audience with the king, it seemed well to him to speak what was in the people's minds.

'Your Majesty,' he said; and then stopped wondering how best to put it.

'Well?' said the king.

'Have I your Majesty's permission to speak my mind?'

'So far; yes,' said the king.

Encouraged by this, the chancellor resolved to put the matter plainly.

'In the event of your Majesty's death – ' He coughed and began again. 'If your Majesty ever *should* die,' he said, 'which in any case will not be for many years – if ever – as, I need hardly say, your Majesty's loyal subjects earnestly hope – I mean they hope it will be never. But assuming for the moment – making the sad assumption –'

'You said you wanted to speak your mind,' interrupted the king. 'Is this it?'

'Yes, your Majesty.'

'Then I don't think much of it.'

'Thank you, your Majesty.'

'What you are trying to say is, "Who will be the next king?" '

'Quite so, your Majesty.'

'Ah!' The king was silent for a little. Then he said, 'I can tell you who won't be.'

The chancellor did not seek for information on this point, feeling that in the circumstances the answer was obvious.

'What do you suggest yourself?'

'That your Majesty choose a successor from among the young and the highly-born of the country, putting him to whatever test seems good to your Majesty.'

The king pulled at his beard and frowned.

'There must be not one test, but many tests. Let all, who will, offer themselves, provided only that they are under the age of twenty and are well born. See to it.'

He waved his hand in dismissal, and with an accuracy established by long practice the chancellor retired backwards out of the palace.

On the following morning, therefore, it was announced that all those who were ambitious to be appointed the king's successor, and who were of high birth and not yet come to the age of twenty, should present themselves a week later for the tests to which his Majesty desired to put them, the first of which would be a running race. Whereat the people rejoiced, for they wished to be ruled by one to whom they could look up, and running was much esteemed in that country.

On the appointed day the excitement was great. All along the course, which was once round the castle, large crowds were massed, and at the finishing point the king and queen themselves were seated in a specially erected pavilion. And to this the competitors were brought to be introduced to their Majesties. There were nine young nobles, well-built and handsome, and (it was thought) intelligent, who were competitors. And there was also one Rabbit.

The chancellor had first noticed the Rabbit when he was lining up the competitors, pinning numbers on their backs so that the people should identify them, and giving them such instructions as seemed necessary to him. 'Now, now, be off with you,' he said, 'Competitors only, this way.' And he had made a motion of impatient dismissal with his foot.

'I *am* a competitor,' said the Rabbit. 'And I don't think it is usual,' he added with dignity, 'for the starter to kick one of the competitors just at the beginning of an important foot-race. It looks like favouritism.'

'*You* can't be a competitor,' laughed all the nobles.

'Why not? Read the rules.'

The chancellor, feeling rather hot suddenly, read the rules. The Rabbit was certainly under twenty; he had a

'This,' said the Chancellor,
as airily as he could,
'is Rabbit'

pedigree which showed that he was of the highest birth; and –

'And,' said the Rabbit, 'I am ambitious to be appointed the king's successor. Those were all the conditions. Now let's get on with the race.'

But first came the introduction to the king. One by one the competitors came up . . . and at the end –

'This,' said the chancellor, as airily as he could, 'is Rabbit.'

Rabbit bowed in the most graceful manner possible; first to the king and then to the queen. But the king only stared at him. Then he turned to the chancellor.

'Well?'

The chancellor shrugged his shoulders. 'His entry does not appear to lack validity,' he said.

'He means, your Majesty, that it is all right,' explained Rabbit.

The king laughed suddenly. 'Go on,' he said. 'We can always have a race for a new chancellor afterwards.'

So the race was started. And the young Lord Calomel

The race was started

was much cheered on coming in second; not only by their Majesties, but also by Rabbit, who had finished the course some time before, and was now lounging in the royal pavilion.

'A very good style, your Majesty,' said Rabbit, turning to the king. 'Altogether he seems to be a most promising youth.'

'Most,' said the king grimly. 'So much so that I do not propose to trouble the rest of the competitors. The next test shall take place between you and him.'

'Not racing again, please, your Majesty. That would hardly be fair to his lordship.'

'No, not racing; fighting.'

'Ah! What sort of fighting?'

'With swords,' said the king.

'I am a little rusty with swords, but I daresay in a day or two – '

'It will be now,' said the king.

'You mean, your Majesty, as soon as Lord Calomel has recovered his breath?'

The king answered nothing, but turned to his chancellor.

'Tell the young Lord Calomel that in half an hour I desire him to fight with this Rabbit – '

'The young Lord Rabbit,' murmured the other competitor to the chancellor.

'To fight with him for my kingdom.'

'*And* borrow me a sword, will you?' said Rabbit. 'Quite a small one. I don't want to hurt him.'

So, half an hour later, on a level patch of grass in front of the pavilion, the fight began. It was a short but exciting struggle. Calomel, whirling his long sword in his strong right arm, dashed upon Rabbit, and Rabbit, carrying his short sword in his teeth, dodged between Calomel's legs and brought him toppling. And when it was seen that the young lord rose from the ground with a broken arm, and that with the utmost gallantry he had now taken his sword in his left hand, the people cheered. And Rabbit, dropping his sword for a moment, cheered too; and then he picked it up and got it entangled in his adversary's legs again, so that again the young Lord Calomel crashed to the ground, this time with a sprained ankle. And there he lay.

Rabbit trotted into the royal pavilion, and dropped his sword in the chancellor's lap.

'Thank you so much,' he said. 'Have I won?'

And the king frowned and pulled at his beard.

'There are other tests,' he muttered.

But what were they to be? It was plain that Lord Calomel was in no condition for another physical test. What, then, of an intellectual test?

'After all,' said the king to the queen that night, 'intelligence is a quality not without value to a ruler.'

'Is it?' asked the queen doubtfully.

'I have found it so,' said the king, a trifle haughtily.

'Oh,' said the queen.

'There is a riddle, of which my father was fond, the

Lord Calomel crashed to the ground

answer to which has never been revealed save to the Royal House. We might make this the final test between them.'

'What is the riddle?'

'I fancy it goes like this.' He thought for a moment, and then recited it, beating time with his hand.

> My *first* I do for your delight,
> Although 'tis neither black nor white.
> My *second* looks the other way,
> Yet always goes to bed by day.
> My *whole* can fly, and climb a tree,
> And sometimes swims upon the sea.

'What is the answer?' asked the queen.

'As far as I remember,' said his Majesty, 'it is either *Dormouse* or *Raspberry*.'

' "Dormouse" doesn't make sense,' objected the queen.

'Neither does "raspberry," ' pointed out the king.

'Then how can they guess it?'

'They can't. But my idea is that young Calomel should be secretly told beforehand what the answer is, so that he may win the competition.'

'Is that fair?' asked the queen doubtfully.

'Yes,' said the king. 'Certainly. Or I wouldn't have suggested it.'

So it was duly announced by the chancellor that the final test between the young Lord Calomel and Rabbit would be the solving of an ancient riddle-me-ree, which in the past had baffled all save those of royal blood. Copies of the riddle had been sent to the competitors, and in a week from that day they would be called upon to give their answers before their Majesties and the full court. And with Lord Calomel's copy went a message, which said this:

'*From a Friend*. The answer is *Dormouse*. BURN THIS.'

The day came round; and Calomel and Rabbit were

brought before their Majesties; and they bowed to their Majesties, and were ordered to be seated, for Calomel's ankle was still painful to him. And when the chancellor had called for silence, the king addressed those present, explaining the conditions of the test to them.

'And the answer to the riddle,' he said, 'is in this sealed paper, which I now hand to my chancellor, in order that he shall open it, as soon as the competitors have told us what they know of the matter.'

The people, being uncertain what else to do, cheered slightly.

'I will ask Lord Calomel first,' his Majesty went on. He looked at his lordship, and his lordship nodded slightly. And Rabbit, noticing that nod, smiled to himself.

The young Lord Calomel tried to look very wise, and he said –

'There are many possible answers to this riddle-me-ree, but the best answer seems to me to be *Dormouse*.'

'Let some one take a note of that answer,' said the king: whereupon the chief secretary wrote down: 'LORD CALOMEL – *Dormouse*.'

'Now,' said the king to Rabbit, 'what suggestion have you to make in this matter?'

Rabbit, who had spent an anxious week inventing answers each more impossible than the last, looked down modestly.

'Well?' said the king.

'Your Majesty,' said the Rabbit with some apparent hesitation, 'I have a great respect for the intelligence of the young Lord Calomel, but I think that in this matter he is mistaken. The answer is not, as he suggests, *woodlouse*, but *dormouse*.'

'I *said* "dormouse," ' cried Calomel indignantly.

'I thought you said "wood-louse," ' said the Rabbit in surprise.

'He certainly said "dormouse," ' said the king coldly.

' "Wood-louse," I *think*,' said Rabbit.

'Lord Calomel – *Dormouse*,' read out the chief secretary.

'There you are,' said Calomel. 'I did say "dormouse." '

'My apologies,' said Rabbit, with a bow. 'Then we are both right, for *dormouse* it certainly is.'

The chancellor broke open the sealed paper, and to the amazement of nearly all present read out, 'Dormouse.'

'Apparently, your Majesty,' he said in some surprise, 'they are both equally correct.'

The king scowled. In some way, which he didn't quite understand, he had been tricked.

'May I suggest, your Majesty,' the chancellor went on, 'that they be asked now some question of a different order, such as can be answered, after not more than a few minutes' thought, here in your Majesty's presence? Some problem in the higher mathematics, for instance, such as might be profitable for a future king to know.'

'What question?' asked his Majesty, a little nervously.

'Well, as an example – what is seven times six?' And, behind his hand, he whispered to the king, 'Forty-two.'

Not a muscle of the king's face moved, but he looked thoughtfully at the Lord Calomel. Supposing his lordship did not know!

'They are both equally correct!'

'Well?' he said reluctantly. 'What is the answer?'

The young Lord Calomel thought for some time, and then said, 'Fifty-four.'

'And you?' said the king to Rabbit.

Rabbit wondered what to say. As long as he gave the same answers as Calomel, he could not lose in the encounter, yet in this case 'forty-two' was the right answer. But the king, who could do no wrong, even in arithmetic, might decide, for the purposes of the competition, that 'fifty-four' was an answer more becoming to the future ruler of the country. Was it, then, safe to say 'Forty-two'?

'Your Majesty,' he said, 'there are several possible answers to this extraordinary novel conundrum. At first sight the obvious solution would appear to be 'forty-two.' The objection to this solution is that it lacks originality. I have long felt that a progressive country such as ours might well strike out a new line in the matter. Let us agree that in future seven sixes are 'fifty-four.' But if your Majesty would prefer to cling to the old style of counting, then your Majesty and your Majesty's chancellor would make the answer "forty-two." '

After saying which, Rabbit bowed gracefully, both to their Majesties and to his opponent and sat down again.

The king scratched his head in a puzzled sort of way.

'The correct answer,' he said, 'is, or will be in the future, "fifty-four." '

'Make a note of that,' whispered the chancellor to the chief secretary.

'Lord Calomel guessed this at his first attempt; Rabbit at his second attempt. I therefore declare Lord Calomel the winner.'

'Shame!' said Rabbit.

'Who said that?' cried the king furiously.

Rabbit looked over his shoulder, with the object of identifying the culprit, but was apparently unsuccessful.

'However,' went on the king, 'in order that there

should be no doubt in the minds of my people as to the absolute fairness with which this competition is being conducted, there will be one further test. It happens that a king is often called upon to make speeches and exhortations to his people, and for this purpose the ability to stand evenly upon two legs for a considerable length of time is of much value to him. The next test, therefore, will be – '

But at this point Lord Calomel cleared his throat so loudly that the king had to stop and listen to him.

'Quite so,' said the king. 'The next test, therefore, will be held in a month's time, when his lordship's ankle is healed, and it will be a test to see who can balance himself longest upon two legs only.'

Rabbit lolloped back to his home in the wood, pondering deeply.

Now there was an enchanter who lived in the wood, a man of many magical gifts. He could (it was averred by the countryside) extract coloured ribbons from his mouth, cook plum-puddings in a hat, and produce as many as ten silk handkerchiefs, knotted together, from a twist of paper. And that night, after a simple dinner of salad, Rabbit called upon him.

'Can you,' he said, 'turn a rabbit into a man?'

The enchanter considered this carefully.

'I can,' he said at last, 'turn a plum-pudding into a rabbit.'

'That,' said Rabbit, 'to be frank, would not be a helpful operation.'

'I can turn almost anything into a rabbit,' said the enchanter with growing enthusiasm. 'In fact, I like doing it.'

Then Rabbit had an idea.

'Can you turn a man into a rabbit?'

'I did once. At least I turned a baby into a baby rabbit.'

'When was that?'

'Eighteen years ago. At the court of King Nicodemus.

I was giving an exhibition of my powers to him and his good queen. I asked one of the company to lend me a baby, never thinking for a moment that – The young prince was handed up. I put a red silk handkerchief over him, and waved my hands. Then I took the handkerchief away . . . The queen was very distressed. I tried everything I could, but it was useless. The king was most generous about it. He said that I could keep the rabbit. I carried it about with me for some weeks, but one day it escaped. Dear, dear!' He wiped his eyes gently with a red silk handkerchief.

'Most interesting,' said Rabbit, 'Well, this is what I want you to do.' And they discussed the matter from the beginning.

A month later the great standing competition was to take place. When all was ready, the king rose to make his opening remarks.

'We are now,' he began, 'to make one of the most interesting tests between our two candidates for the throne. At the word "Go!" they will – ' And then he stopped suddenly. 'Why, what's this?' he said, putting on his spectacles. 'Where is the young Lord Calomel? And what is that second rabbit doing? There was no need to bring your brother,' he added severely to Rabbit.

'I am Lord Calomel,' said the second rabbit meekly.

'Oh!' said the king.

'Go!' said the chancellor, who was a little deaf.

Rabbit, who had been practising for a month, jumped on his back paws and remained there. Lord Calomel, who had had no practice at all, remained on all fours. In the crowd at the back the enchanter chuckled to himself.

'How long do I stay like this?' asked Rabbit.

'This is all very awkward and distressing,' said the king.

'May I get down?' said Rabbit.

'There is no doubt that the Rabbit has won,' said the chancellor.

THE BOOK OF ANIMAL STORIES

'Which rabbit?' cried the king crossly. 'They're both rabbits.'

'The one with the white spots behind the ears,' said Rabbit helpfully.

'May I get down?'

There was a sudden cry from the back of the hall.

'Your Majesty?'

'Well, well, what is it?'

The enchanter pushed his way forward.

'May I look, your Majesty?' he said in a trembling voice. 'White spots behind the ears? Dear, dear! Allow me!' He seized Rabbit's ears, and bent them this way and that.

'Ow!' said Rabbit.

'It is! Your Majesty, it is!'

'Is what?'

'The son of the late King Nicodemus, whose country is now joined to your own. Prince Silvio.'

'Quite so,' said Rabbit airily, hiding his surprise. 'Didn't any of you recognize me?'

'Nicodemus only had one son,' said the chancellor, 'and he died as a baby.'

'Not died,' said the enchanter, and forthwith explained the whole sad story.

'I see,' said the king, when the story was ended. 'But of course that is neither here nor there. A competition like this must be conducted with absolute impartiality.' He turned to the chancellor. 'Which of them won that last test?'

'Prince Silvio,' said the chancellor.

'Then, my dear Prince Silvio – '

'One moment,' interrupted the enchanter excitedly. 'I've just thought of the words. I *knew* there were some words you had to say.'

He threw his red silk handkerchief over Rabbit, and cried, 'Hey presto!'

And the handkerchief rose and rose and rose . . .

And there was Prince Silvio!

You can imagine how loudly the people cheered. But the king appeared not to notice that anything surprising had happened.

'Then, my dear Prince Silvio,' he went on, 'as the winner of this most interesting series of contests, you are appointed successor to our throne.'

'Your Majesty,' said Silvio 'this is too much.' And he turned to the enchanter and said, 'May I borrow your handkerchief for a moment? My emotion has overcome me.'

So on the following day, Prince Rabbit was duly proclaimed heir to the throne before all the people. But not until the ceremony was over did he return the enchanter's red handkerchief.

'And now,' he said to the enchanter, 'you may restore Lord Calomel to his proper shape.'

And the enchanter placed his handkerchief on Lord Calomel's head and said, 'Hey presto!' and Lord Calomel stretched himself and said, 'Thanks very much.' But he said it rather coldly, as if he were not really very grateful.

So they all lived happily for a long time. And Prince Rabbit married the most beautiful princess of those parts; and when a son was born to them there was much feasting and jollification. And the king gave a great party, whereat minstrels, tumblers, jugglers, and suchlike were present in large quantities to give pleasure to the company. But in spite of a suggestion made by the princess, the enchanter was not present.

'But I hear he is so clever,' said the princess to her husband.

'He has many amusing inventions,' replied the prince, 'but some of them are not in the best of taste.'

'Very well, dear,' said the princess.

The Jungle

by E. Nesbit

'CHILDREN are like jam – all very well in the proper place, but you can't stand them all over the shop – eh, what?'

These were the dreadful words of our Indian uncle. They made us feel very young and angry, yet we could not be comforted by calling him names to ourselves, as you do when nasty grown-ups say nasty things, because he is not nasty, but quite the exact opposite when not irritated. And we could not think it ungentlemanly of him to say we were like jam, because, as Alice says, jam is very nice indeed – only not on furniture and improper places like that. My father said, 'Perhaps they had better go to boarding-school.' And that was awful, because we know father disapproves of boarding-schools. And he looked at us and said, 'I am ashamed of them, sir!'

Your lot is indeed a dark and terrible one when your father is ashamed of you. And we all knew this, so that we felt in our chests just as if we had swallowed a hard-boiled egg whole. At least, this is what Oswald felt, and father said once that Oswald, as the eldest, was the representative of the family, so, of course, the others felt the same.

And then everybody said nothing for a short time. At last father said, 'You may go, but remember –' The words that followed I am not going to tell you. It is no use telling you what you knew before – as they do in schools. And you must all have had such words said to you many times. We went away when it was over. The girls cried, and we boys got out books and began to read, so that nobody should think we cared. But we felt it deeply in our interior hearts, especially Oswald, who is the eldest and the representative of the family.

We felt it all the more because we had not really meant to do anything wrong. We only thought perhaps the grown-ups would not be quite pleased if they knew, and that is quite different. Besides we meant to put all the things back in their proper places when we had done with them before any one found out about it. But I must not anticipate (that means telling the end of a story before the beginning. I tell you this because it is so sickening to have words you don't know in a story, and to be told to look it up in the dicker).

We are the Bastables – Oswald, Dora, Dickie, Alice, Noël, and H.O. If you want to know why we call our youngest brother H.O. you can jolly well read *The Treasure Seekers*, and find out. We were the treasure seekers, and we sought it high and low, and quite regularly, because we particularly wanted to find it. And at last we did not find it, but we were found by a good, kind Indian uncle, who helped father with his business, so that father was able to take us to live in a jolly big red house on Blackheath, instead of in the Lewisham Road, where we lived when we were only poor but honest treasure seekers. When we were poor but honest we always used to think that if only father had plenty of business, we did not have to go short of pocket-money and wear shabby clothes (I don't mind this myself but the girls do), we should be quite happy and very, very good.

And when we were taken to the beautiful big Black-heath house we thought now all would be well, because it was a house with vineries and pineries, and gas and water, and shrubberies and stabling, and replete with every modern convenience, like it says in Dyer and Hilton's list of Eligible House Property. I read all about it, and I have copied the words quite right.

It is a beautiful house, all the furniture solid and strong, no casters off the chairs, and the tables not scratched, and the silver not dented; and lots of servants, and the most decent meals every day – and lots of pocket-money.

But it is wonderful how soon you get used to things, even the things you want most. Our watches, for in-stance. We wanted them frightfully; but when I had had mine a week or two, after the mainspring got broken and was repaired at Bennett's in the village, I hardly cared to look at the works at all, and it did not make me feel happy in my heart any more, though, of course, I should have been very unhappy if it had been taken away from me. And the same with new clothes and nice dinners and having enough of everything. You soon get used to it all, and it does not make you extra happy, although, if you had it all taken away you would be very dejected. (That is a good word, and one I have never used before.) You get used to everything, as I said, and then you want something more.

Father says this is what people mean by the deceitful-ness of riches; but Albert's uncle says it is the spirit of progress, and Mrs. Leslie said some people called it 'divine discontent.' Oswald asked them all what they thought one Sunday at dinner. Uncle said it was rot, and what we wanted was bread and water and a licking; but he meant it for a joke. This was in the Easter holidays.

We went to live at the Red House at Christmas. After

the holidays the girls went to the Blackheath High
School, and we boys went to the Prop. (that means the
Proprietary School). And we had to swot rather during
term; but about Easter we knew the deceitfulness of
riches in the vac., when there was nothing much on, like
pantomimes and things. Then there was the summer
term, and we swotted more than ever; and it was boiling
hot, and masters' tempers got short and sharp, and the
girls used to wish the exams came in cold weather. I can't
think why they don't. But I suppose schools don't think
of sensible things like that. They teach botany at girls'
schools.

Then the midsummer holidays came, and we breathed again – but only for a few days. We began to feel as if
we had forgotten something, and did not know what it
was. We wanted something to happen – only we didn't
exactly know what. So we were very pleased when father
said – 'I've asked Mr. Foulkes to send his children here
for a week or two. You know – the kids who came at
Christmas. You must be jolly to them, and see that they
have a good time, don't you know.'

We remembered them right enough – they were like
pinky, frightened things, like white mice, with very
bright eyes. They had not been to our house since
Christmas, because Denis, the boy, had been ill, and they
had been with an aunt at Ramsgate.

Alice and Dora would have liked to get the bedrooms
ready for the honoured guests, but a really good housemaid is sometimes more ready to say 'Don't' than even a
general. So the girls had to chuck it. Jane only let them
put flowers in the pots on the visitors' mantlepieces, and
then they had to ask the gardener which kind they might
pick, because nothing worth gathering happened to be
growing in our own gardens just then.

Their train got in at 12.27. We all went to meet them.
Afterwards I thought that was a mistake, because their
aunt was with them, and she wore black with beady

things and a tight bonnet, and she said, when we took our hats off –

'Who are you?' quite crossly.

We said, 'We are the Bastables; we've come to meet Daisy and Denny.'

The aunt is a very rude lady, and it made us sorry for Daisy and Denny when she said to them –

'*Are* these the children? Do you remember them?'

We weren't very tidy, perhaps, because we'd been playing brigands in the shrubbery; and we knew we should have to wash for dinner as soon as we got back, anyhow. But still –

Denny said he thought he remembered us. But Daisy said, 'Of course they are,' and then looked as if she were going to cry.

So then the aunt called a cab, and told the man where to drive, and put Daisy and Denny in, and then she said, 'You two little girls may go too, if you like, but you little boys must walk.'

So the cab went off, and we were left. The aunt turned to us to say a few last words. We knew it would have been about brushing your hair and wearing gloves, so Oswald said, 'Good-bye,' and turned haughtily away, before she could begin, and so did the others. No one but that kind of black beady tight lady would say 'little boys.' She is like Miss Murdstone in *David Copperfield*. I should like to tell her so; but she would not understand. I don't suppose she has ever read anything but *Markham's History* and *Magnall's Questions* – improving books like that.

When we got home we found all four of those who had ridden in the cab in our sitting-room – we don't call it nursery now – looking very thoroughly washed, and our girls were asking polite questions and the others were saying 'yes' and 'no,' and 'I don't know.' We boys did not say anything. We just stood at the window and looked out till the gong went for our dinner.

We felt it was going to be awful – and it was. The

newcomers would never have done for knight-errants, or to carry the cardinal's sealed message through the heart of France on a horse; they would never have thought of anything to say to throw the enemy off the scent when they got into a tight place.

They said 'Yes, please,' and 'No, thank you'; and they ate very neatly, and always wiped their mouths before they drank, as well as after, and never spoke with them full.

And after dinner it got worse and worse.

We got out all our books, and they said, 'Thank you,' and didn't look at them properly. And we got out all our toys, and they said, 'Thank you, it's very nice,' to everything. And it got less and less pleasant, and towards tea-time it came to nobody saying anything except Noël and H.O. – and they talked to each other about cricket.

After tea father came in, and he played 'Letters' with them and the girls, and it was a little better; but while late dinner was going on – I shall never forget it. Oswald felt like the hero of a book – 'almost at the end of his resources.' I don't think I was ever glad of bedtime before, but that time I was.

When they had gone to bed (Daisy had to have all her strings and buttons undone for her, Dora told me, though she is nearly ten, and Denny said he couldn't sleep without the gas being left a little bit on) we held a council in the girls' room. We all sat on the bed – it is a mahogany four-poster with green curtains, very good for tents, only the housekeeper doesn't allow it – and Oswald said –

'This is jolly nice, isn't it?'

'They'll be better tomorrow,' Alice said, 'they're only shy.'

Dickie said shy was all very well, but you needn't behave like a perfect idiot.

'They're frightened. You see we're all strange to them,' Dora said.

'We're not wild beasts or Indians; we shan't eat them. What have they got to be frightened of?' Dickie said this.

Noël told us he thought they were an enchanted prince and princess who'd been turned into white rabbits, and their bodies had got changed back, but not their insides.

But Oswald told him to dry up. 'It's no use making things up about them,' he said. 'The thing is: what are we going to *do*? We can't have our holidays spoiled by these snivelling kids.'

'No,' Alice said, 'but they can't possibly go on snivelling for ever. Perhaps they've got into the habit of it with that Murdstone aunt. She's enough to make any one snivel.'

'All the same,' said Oswald, 'we jolly well aren't going to have another day like today. We must do something to rouse them from their snivelling leth – what's its name? – something sudden and – what is it? decisive.'

'A booby-trap,' said H.O., 'the first thing when they get up, and an apple-pie bed at night.'

But Dora would not hear of it, and I own she was right.

'Suppose,' she said, 'we could get up a good play – like we did when we were treasure seekers.'

We said, 'Well, what?' But she did not say.

'It ought to be a good long thing – to last all day,' Dickie said: 'and if they like they can play, and if they don't –'

'If they don't, I'll read to them,' Alice said.

But we all said, 'No, you don't – if you begin that way, you'll have to go on.' And Dickie added, 'I wasn't going to say that at all. I was going to say if they didn't like it they could jolly well do the other thing.'

We all agreed that we must think of something, but we none of us could, and at last the council broke up in confusion, because Mrs. Blake – she is the housekeeper – came up and turned off the gas.

But next morning when we were having breakfast, and the two strangers were sitting there so pink and clean, Oswald suddenly said –

'I know; we'll have a jungle in the garden.'

And the others agreed, and we talked about it till brek was over. The little strangers only said, 'I don't know,' whenever we said anything to them.

After brekker, Oswald beckoned his brothers and sisters apart, and said, 'Do you agree to let me be captain today, because I thought of it?'

And they said they would.

Then he said, 'We'll play jungle book, and I shall be Mowgli. The rest of you can be what you like – Mowgli's father and mother, or any of the beasts.'

'I don't suppose they know the book,' said Noël. 'They don't look as if they read anything, except at lesson times.'

'Then they can go on being beasts all the time,' Oswald said. 'Any one can be a beast.'

So it was settled.

And now Oswald – Albert's uncle has sometimes said he is clever at arranging things – began to lay his plans for the jungle. The day was well chosen. Our Indian uncle was away, father was away, Mrs. Blake was going away, and the housemaid had an afternoon off. Oswald's first conscious act was to get rid of the white mice – I mean the little good visitors. He explained to them that there would be a play in the afternoon, and they could be what they liked, and gave them the jungle book to read the stories he told them to – all the ones about Mowgli. He led the strangers to a secluded spot among the sea-kale pots in the kitchen garden and left them. Then he went back to the others, and we had a jolly morning under the cedar talking about what we would do when Blakie was gone. She took her departure just after our dinner.

When we asked Denny what he would like to be in the

play, it turned out he had not read the stories Oswald told him at all, but only the 'White Seal' and 'Rikki Tikki.'

We then agreed to make the jungle first and dress up for our parts afterwards. Oswald was a little uncomfortable about leaving the strangers alone all the morning, so he said Denny should be his aide-de-camp, and he was really quite useful. He is rather handy with his fingers, and things that he does up do not come untied. Daisy might have come too, but she wanted to go on reading, so we let her, which is the truest manners to a visitor. Of course the shrubbery was to be the jungle, and the lawn under the cedar a forest glade, and then we began to collect the things. The cedar lawn is just nicely out of the way of the windows. It was a jolly hot day – the kind of day when the sunshine is white and the shadows are dark grey, not black like they are in the evening.

We all thought of different things. Of course first we dressed up pillows in the skins of beasts, and set them about on the grass to look as natural as we could. And then we got Pincher, and rubbed him all over with powdered slate pencil, to make him the right colour for Grey Brother. But he shook it all off, and it had taken an awful time to do. Then Alice said – 'Oh, I know!' and she ran off to father's dressing-room, and came back with the tube of *crême d'amande pour la barbe et les mains*, and we squeezed it on Pincher and rubbed it in, and then the slate pencil stuff stuck all right, and he rolled in the dust-bin of his own accord, which made him just the right colour. He is a very clever dog, but soon after we went off and we did not find him till quite late in the afternoon. Denny helped with Pincher, and with the wild-beast skins, and when Pincher was finished, he said –

'Please, may I make some paper birds to put in the trees? I know how.'

And, of course, we said 'Yes,' and he only had red ink and newspapers, and quickly he made quite a lot of large paper birds with red tails. They didn't look half bad on the edge of the shrubbery.

While he was doing this he suddenly said, or rather screamed, 'Oh!'

And we looked, and it was a creature with great horns and a fur rug – something like a bull and something like a minotaur – and I don't wonder Denny was frightened. It was Alice, and it was first-class.

Up to now all was not yet lost beyond recall. It was the stuffed fox that did the mischief – and I am sorry to own it was Oswald who thought of it. He is not ashamed of having *thought* of it. That was rather clever of him. But he knows now that it is better not to take other people's foxes and things without asking, even if you live in the same house with them.

It was Oswald who undid the back of the glass case in the hall and got out the fox with the green and grey duck in its mouth, and when the others saw how awfully like life they looked on the lawn, they all rushed off to fetch the other stuffed things. Uncle has a tremendous

The fox with the green and grey duck in its mouth

lot of stuffed things. He shot most of them himself – but not the fox, of course. There was another fox's mask, too, and we hung that in a bush to look as if the fox was peeping out. And the stuffed birds we fastened on to the trees with string. The duck-bill – what's its other name? – looked very well sitting on his tail with the otter snarling at him. Then Dickie had an idea; and though not nearly so much was said about it afterwards as there was about the stuffed things, I think myself it was just as bad, though it was a good idea too. He just got the hose and put the end over a branch of the cedar tree. Then we got the steps they clean windows with, and let the hose rest on the top of the steps and run. It was to be a waterfall, but it ran between the steps and was only wet and messy; so we got father's mackintosh and uncle's and covered the steps with them, so that the water ran down all right and was glorious, and it ran away in a stream across the grass where we had dug a little channel for it – and the otter and the duck-bill thing were as if in their native haunts. I hope all this is not very dull to read about. I know it was jolly good fun to do. Taking one thing with another, I don't know that we ever had a better time while it lasted.

We got all the rabbits out of the hutches and put pink paper tails on to them, and hunted them with horns made out of the *Times*. They got away somehow, and before they were caught next day they had eaten a good many lettuces and other things. Oswald is very sorry for this. He rather likes the gardener.

Denny wanted to put paper tails on the guinea-pig, and it was no use our telling him there was nothing to tie the paper on to. He thought we were kidding until we showed him, and then he said, 'Well, never mind,' and got the girls to give him bits of the blue stuff left over from their dressing-gowns.

'I'll make them sashes to tie around their little mid-dles,' he said. And he did, and the bows stuck up on the

Rabbits with pink paper tails

tops of their backs. One of the guinea-pigs was never seen again, and the same with the tortoise when we had done his shell with vermilion paint. He crawled away, and returned no more. Perhaps someone collected him and thought he was an expensive kind of unknown in these cold latitudes.

The lawn under the cedar was transformed into a dream of beauty, what with the stuffed creatures and the paper-tailed things and the waterfall. And Alice said –

'I wish the tigers did not look so flat.' For, of course, with pillows you can only pretend it is a sleeping tiger getting ready to make a spring out at you. It is difficult to prop up tiger-skins in a lifelike manner when there are no bones inside them, only pillows and sofa cushions. 'What about the beer-stands?' I said. And we got two out of the cellar. With bolsters and string we fastened insides to the tigers – and they were really fine. The legs of the beer-stands did for tiger's legs. It was indeed the finishing touch.

Then we boys put on just our bathing drawers and vests – so as to be able to play with the waterfall without hurting our clothes. I think this was thoughtful. The girls only tucked up their frocks and took their shoes and stockings off. H.O. painted his legs and his hands with Condy's fluid – to make him brown, so that he might be Mowgli, although Oswald was captain and had plainly said he was going to be Mowgli himself. Of course the others weren't going to stand that. So Oswald said –

'Very well. Nobody asked you to brown yourself like that. But now you've done it, you've simply got to go and be a beaver, and live in the dam under the waterfall till it washes off.'

He said he didn't want to be a beaver.

And Noël said, 'Don't make him. Let him be the bronze statue in the palace gardens that the fountain plays out of.'

So we let him have the hose and hold it up over his head. It made a lovely fountain, only he remained brown. So then Dickie and Oswald did ourselves brown too, and dried H.O. as well as we could with our handkerchiefs, because he was just beginning to snivel. The brown did not come off any of us for days.

Oswald was to be Mowgli, and we were just beginning to arrange the different parts. The rest of the hose that was on the ground was Kaa, the rock python, and Pincher was grey brother, only we couldn't find him. And while most of us were talking, Dickie and Noël got messing about with the beer-stand tigers.

And then a really sad event instantly occurred, which was not really our fault, and we did not mean to.

That Daisy girl had been mooning indoors all the afternoon with the jungle books, and now she came suddenly out, just as Dickie and Noël had got under the tigers and were shoving them along to fright each other. Of course, this is not in the Mowgli book at all; but they did look jolly like real tigers, and I am very far from wishing to blame the girl, though she little knew what would be the awful consequences of her rash act. But for her we might have got out of it all much better than we did.

What happened was truly horrid.

As soon as Daisy saw the tigers she stopped short, and uttering a shriek like a railway whistle, she fell flat on the ground.

'Fear not, gentle Indian maiden,' Oswald cried, thinking with surprise that perhaps after all she did know how to play. 'I myself will protect thee.' And he sprung forward with the native bow and arrows out of uncle's study.

The gentle Indian maiden did not move.

'Come hither,' Dora said, 'let us take refuge in yonder covert while this good knight does battle for us.'

Dora might have remembered that we were savages, but she did not. And that is Dora all over. And still the Daisy girl did not move.

Then we were truly frightened. Dora and Alice lifted her up, and her mouth was a horrid violet colour and her eyes half-shut. She looked horrid. Not at all like fair fainting damsels, who are always of an interesting pallor. She was green, like a cheap oyster on a stall.

We did what we could, a prey to alarm as we were. We rubbed her hands and let the hose play gently but perseveringly on her unconscious brow. The girls loosened her dress, though it was only the kind that comes down straight without a waist. And we were all doing what we could as hard as we could, when we heard the click of the front gate. There was no mistake about it.

'I hope whoever it is will go straight to the front door,' said Alice. But whoever it was did not. There were feet on the gravel, and there was uncle's voice, saying in his hearty manner –

'This way. This way. On such a day as this we shall find our young barbarians all at play somewhere about the grounds.'

And then, without further warning, the uncle, three other gentlemen, and two ladies burst upon the scene.

We had no clothes on to speak of – I mean us boys. We were all wet through. Daisy was in a faint or a fit, or dead – none of us knew which. And all the stuffed animals were there staring the uncle in the face. Most of them had got a sprinkling, and the otter and the duck-bill brute were simply soaked. And three of us were dark brown. Concealment, as so often happens, was impossible.

The quick brain of Oswald saw, in a flash, exactly how it would strike the uncle, and his brave young blood ran cold in his veins. His heart stood still.

'What's all this – eh, what?' said the tones of the wronged uncle.

Oswald spoke up and said it was jungles we were playing, and he didn't know what was up with Daisy. He explained as well as any one could, but words were now in vain.

The uncle had a malacca cane in his hand, and we were but ill-prepared to meet the sudden attack. Oswald and H.O. caught it worst. The other boys were under the tigers – and, of course, my uncle would not strike a girl. Denny was a visitor and so got off. But it was bread and water for us for the next three days, and our own rooms. I will not tell you how we sought to vary the monotonousness of imprisonment. Oswald thought of taming a mouse, but he could not find one. The reason of the wretched captives might have given way but for the gutter that you can crawl along from our room to the girls'. But I will not dwell on this because you might try it yourselves, and it really is dangerous. When my father came home we got the talking to, and we said we were sorry – and we really were – especially about Daisy, though she had behaved with muffishness, and then it was settled that we were to go into the country and stay till we had grown into better children.

Albert's uncle was writing a book in the country; we were to go to his house. We were glad of this – Daisy and Denny too. This we bore nobly. We knew we had deserved it. We were all very sorry for everything, and we resolved that for the future we *would* be good.

I am not sure whether we kept this resolution or not. Oswald thinks now that perhaps we made a mistake in trying so very hard to be good all at once. You should do everything by degrees.

P.S. – It turned out Daisy was not really dead at all. It was only fainting – so like a girl.

N.B. – Pincher was found on the drawing-room sofa.

Appendix. – I have not told you half the things we did for the jungle – for instance, about the elephants' tusks and the horse-hair sofa cushions, and uncle's fishing-boots.

Lassie Comes Over the Border

from *Lassie Come Home*
by Eric Knight

SLOWLY, steadily, Lassie came across a field.
She was not trotting now. She was going at a painful walk. Her head was low and her tail hung lifelessly. Her thin body moved from side to side as though it took the effort of her entire frame to make her legs continue to function.

But her course was straight. She was still continuing to go south.

Across the meadow she came in her tired walk. She paid no attention to the cattle that grazed on the green about her and that lifted their heads from their feeding to regard her as she passed.

The grass grew thicker and coarser as she followed the path. The track became beaten mud. Then the mud was a puddle of water and the puddle was the edge of a river.

She stood at the trampled place. It was where the cattle came to drink and to stand for coolness in the heat of the day. Beyond her some of them stood now, knee-deep in the slow backwater. They turned and regarded her, their jaws moving unceasingly.

Lassie whimpered slightly and lifted her head as if to catch some scent from the far bank. She rocked on her feet a moment. Then, wading forward tentatively, she went deeper and deeper. Her feet now felt no bottom. The backwater began to carry her upstream. She began swimming, her tail swirling out behind her.

This was not a turbulent river like the one back in the Highlands. It was not a dirty, factory-clustered one like that now many miles back in the industrial city. But it was broad, and its current went firmly, carrying Lassie downstream.

Her tired legs drove with the beat, her forefeet pumped steadily. The south bank moved past her, but she seemed to be getting no nearer.

Weakness numbed her, and her beat grew slower. Her outstretched head came under the water. As if this wakened her from a sleep, she began threshing wildly. Her head went straight up, and her forefeet sent a splashing foam before her. She was a swimmer in panic.

But her head cleared again, and once more she settled down to the steady drive forward.

It was a long swim – a courageous swim. And when at last she reached the other shore, she was almost too weak to climb the bank. At the first place, her forepaws scratched and she fell back. The bank was too high. The backwater began carrying her upstream. Lassie tried again. She splashed and fell back again. Then the eddy carried her, and at last her feet touched a shelving bottom. She waded to shore.

As though the weight of the water in her coat were an extra load that was too much for her to carry, she staggered. Then dragging herself rather than walking, she crawled up the bank. And there, at last, she dropped. She could go no further.

But she was in England! Lassie did not know that. She was only a dog going home – not a human being wise in the manner of maps. She could not know that she had made her way all down through the Highlands, the Lowlands; that the river she had crossed was the Tweed, which divides England from Scotland.

All these things she did not know. All she knew was that, as she crawled higher on the bank, a strange thing happened. Her legs would no longer respond properly, and, as she was urging herself forward, the tired muscles rebelled at last. She sank, plunged a moment, and then fell on her side.

For a second, she whined. With her forepaws she clawed the earth, still dragging herself South. She was in rough grass now. She pulled herself along – a yard – another foot – another few inches. Then at last the muscles stopped their work.

Lassie lay on one side, her legs outstretched in 'dead dog' position. Her eyes were glazed. The only movement was a spasmodic lifting and falling of the pinched flanks.

All that day Lassie lay there. The flies buzzed about her, but she did not lift her head to snap at them.

Evening came, and across the river was the sound of the herder and the lowing of the cows. The last notes of the birds came – the singing of a thrush through the lingering twilight.

Darkness came with its night sounds, the scream of an owl and the stealthy rippling of a hunting otter, the faraway bark of a farm dog, and the whispering in the trees.

Dawn came with new sounds – the splash of a leaping trout while the river was still veiled in mist. Then the rooks rose with their eternal cry of warning as a man left the door of the farm cottage over the fields. The sun came, and the shadows danced weakly on the grass as the overhead trees shimmered in the first breeze of the new day.

As the sun reached her, Lassie rose slowly. Her eyes were dull. Walking slowly, she set out – away from the river, going south.

The room was small and humble. In a chair beside a table where the lamp glowed, Daniel Fadden sat, reading slowly from the newspaper. Nearer the coal fire on the hearth, his wife sat in a rocking chair, knitting. She teetered endlessly back and forth as her fingers flashed over the wool and needles, so that the movements all seemed related – one rock of the chair, three stitches on the needles.

They were both old people, and it seemed that they had been so long together in life that there was no longer any need to talk. They were contented just to be, sure in the knowledge the other was near.

Finally the man pushed his steel-rimmed spectacles back on his forehead and looked at the hearth.

'We'll do wi' a bit more coal on the fire,' he said.

His wife nodded as she rocked, and her lips went through the noiseless form of counting. She was 'turning a heel' in her knitting and wanted to keep sure count.

The man rose slowly. Taking the scuttle, he went to the sink. In the cupboard beneath was the coal bin. With a little shovel he slowly scooped some out.

'Ah, we're nearly oot,' he said.

His wife looked over. Mentally both of them began to count – the cost of more coal. How quickly they had used the last hundredweight. Their lives were deeply concerned with these things. Expenses ran very close. All they had was the small pension that they received for their son who had been killed in France. Then each of them drew the old-age pension of ten shillings a week given by the State. This was no wealth, but they husbanded it carefully and owed no man. The tiny cottage, far out on the highway from any town, was a cheap place to live. In the little plot of land about it, Fadden grew a stock of vegetables. He had a flock of chickens, several ducks and a goose 'fattening for Christmas'. This last was their largest and most lasting joke. Some years before Fadden had traded a dozen early hen eggs for one tiny gosling. Carefully he had raised it, boasting about what a fine plump bird it would be by Christmas time.

It had become just that – marvellous and plump. And a few days before the holiday of holidays, Fadden had taken his hatchet, and he had sat indoors a long time, regarding it. Finally his wife, understanding, had looked up patiently.

'Dan,' she said. 'I just don't think I'd favour goose this year. If you did a chicken instead – and . . .'

'Aye, Dally,' Fadden had said. 'It would be a terrible waste – one big goose for just the two on us. Now a chicken would be just right . . .'

And so the goose was spared. Each year after that it was dutifully fattened for Christmas.

'This year it goes,' Fadden would always announce. 'Fattening a goose all year, just to strut and waddle round like he's king of everything. This year he goes.'

And always the goose lived. His wife always knew it would. When Fadden announced belligerently that it was headed for the Yule oven, she would say dutifully, 'Aye, Dan.' And when he hemmed and hawed at the last minute and announced that a goose was much too big for the two of them, she would say, 'Aye, Dan.' Privately she often said to herself that the goose would be living long after, as she put it, the two of them were 'deep under the ground and at rest'.

But she would not have it otherwise. In fact, if Dan had ever gone through with his firmly announced intentions, she would have felt the world was dropping from under her.

Of course, it cost a lot to feed up a great, hungry

goose, but one could save other ways. A penny here, a penny there. One could always buy carefully and save carefully, nursing the copper coins along.

So their life went, with dignity and great content – but always with the thought of precious pennies, as it was this evening, when they both reckoned up the amount of coal and how long it had lasted.

'Ah, never mind mending the fire, Dan,' she said. 'Just bed it up wi' ashes and we'll away to bed. We stay up too late anyhow.'

'Sit ye there awhile,' Daniel said, for he knew Dally dearly loved to rock and knit before the hearth for a couple of hours in the evening. 'It's early yet. I'll put just a little on. For Heaven knows, it's chilly enough tonight – nasty, cold, east rain.'

Dally nodded. As she rocked she listened to the wind howling at the east of the low house and the slatting of the rain on the shutters.

'It'll be coming up for autumn soon, Dan.'

'Aye, that it will. This is the first o' them easters. And cold! Blaw right through a man's body to his bones. I'd hate to be oot in it long.'

His wife rocked steadily, and her mind wandered. Whenever anyone talked of bad weather, she always turned her mind back to young Dannie. In those trenches they had had no warm hearths. The men had lived their lives that first winter in muddy holes in the ground – sleeping there of nights with no shelter. A body would die, you would think. And yet, when Dannie had come home on leave, there he was all glowing and healthy and fine. And when she'd asked him about being careful to keep his chest warm and his throat dry, he had laughed and held his sides – a big, booming, strong laugh.

'Eigh, after living through this winter i' France, it's never cold that'll carry me off, Ma,' he boomed.

And it wasn't cold nor illness. Machine guns, his Colonel had written in the letter that Dally still kept folded away beside her marriage lines.

Ah, war – machine wars. Bullets took them all. The brave and the cowardly, the weak and the fine strong ones like Dannie. And it wasn't the dying that took bravery, then, for cowards could die. It was the living that took bravery – living in that mud and rain and cold and keeping the spirit strong through it all. That was the bravery. And how often she pictured it, when the winds blew and the cold rain slatted. All so long ago, but she still pictured it, knitting, purling, rocking – knitting, purling, rocking.

She halted her chair and sat with head erect. For a moment she was still. Then she began again – knitting, purling, rocking, thinking . . .

Again she stopped. She held her breath to hear better – hear above the sound of the fire. There was the hiss of the coal, the spit of ashes dropping in the pit beneath the grate, the crinkle of the newspaper; farther away the tap of a shutter looser than the rest, the surging smacking of rain. Farther beyond that there was another noise, out in the sweep of the wind. Or was it imagination, from thinking of Dannie so long ago?

She dropped her head. Then she sat up again.

'Dan! There's something by the chickens!'

He sat erect a moment.

'Ah now, Dally. Ye're allus imagining things,' he reproved. 'There's not a thing but the wind. And that shutter's a bit loose. I'll have to fix it.'

He went back to his reading, but the little grey-haired woman sat with head erect. Then she spoke again.

'There – again! There is something!'

She rose. 'If you won't go see what's after your chickens, Daniel Fadden, I will!'

She took her shawl, but her husband rose.

'Now, now, now,' he grumbled. 'Sit ye down. If ye want me to go, I'll go just make your soul content. Now I'll look around.'

'Wrap your muffler round your neck first, then,' she reproved.

She watched him go, then she was alone in the house. Her ears, attuned by the lonesomeness to the sounds of living, heard his footsteps go away – and a few moments later, above the noise of the storm, come back quickly. He was running. She jumped up and faced the door before it opened.

'Get your shawl and come,' he said. 'I've found it. Where's the lantern?'

Together they hurried out into the night, leaning against the gusts of wind and rain. Going up the road beside the hawthorn hedge that bordered the highway, at last the old man paused and scrambled down the bank. His wife held up the lantern. There she saw what her husband had found – a dog, lying in the ditch. She watched its head turn, and for a second the light glowed incandescent in its eyes as the lamp shone.

'Puir, puir thing,' she said. 'And who would leave their dog oot a night like this?'

The words were torn away by the wind, but the old man heard the sound of her voice.

'It's too done up to walk,' he shouted. 'Hold the lantern up!'

'Shall I gie ye a hand?'

'Hey?'

She bent down and shouted.

'Shall I gie ye a hand?'

'No! I can manage!'

She saw him bend and pick up the animal. Grasping the shawl against the gale that would pluck it away, she went beside him, holding the lantern high.

'Go easy, Dan, now,' she said. 'Oh, puir, puir thing!'

She ran ahead of him to open the door. Panting, the old man struggled in. The door slammed. The two old people brought Lassie into the warmth of the hearth and laid her on the rug.

They stood back a moment, looking at her. Lassie lay with eyes closed.

'I doubt it'll live till the morn,' the man said.

'Well, that's no reason to stand there. We can at least try. Get your wet things off, quick, Dan, or I'll have you down, too. Look at it shiver – it isn't dead. Get that sack fro' the bottom o' the cupboard, Dan, and dry it off some.'

Awkwardly the old man bent, rubbing the dog's drenched coat.

'She's awful mucky, Dally,' he said. 'Your nice clean hearth rug'll be all muddied up.'

'Then there'll be a job for you shaking it out in the morning,' she answered tartly. 'I wonder if we could feed it?'

The old man looked up. His wife was holding in her hand the can of condensed milk. Their unspoken thoughts went back and forth like a silent conversation. It was the last of their milk.

'Well, we'll have tea for breakfast wi'oot any,' the woman said.

'Save a bit, Dally, ye don't like your tea wi'oot milk.'

'Eigh, it won't matter,' she said.

She began warming the milk in water.

'I often think we just do things fro' habit, Dan,' she went on. 'They say i' China, now, they always drink tea wi'oot milk.'

'Happen it's because they haven't learned any better,' he mumbled.

He kept on rubbing the dog's cold body as his wife stirred the milk in the pan on the grate. There was silence in the cottage.

Lassie lay there, unmoving. In her half-consciousness and terrible weariness, a feeling of dim peace stole over her. So many things came from the past and comforted her. The place smelled 'right'. There was the mixed aroma of coalsmoke and baking bread. The hands that touched her – they did not imprison or bring pain. Instead they soothed and brought peace to sore and aching muscles. The people – they did not move suddenly or shout noisily or throw things that hurt. They went quietly, not startling a dog.

There was warmth, too – this most of all. It was a drugging warmth, one which took the senses away and made awareness slip away as if in a gentle stream that flowed on to forgetfulness and death.

Only dimly Lassie knew of the saucer of warm milk set beside her head. Her senses would not come back from their half-conscious state. She tried to lift her head but it would not move.

Then she felt her head being lifted. The warm milk was being spooned down her throat. She gulped, once – twice – three times. The trickle of hotness went into her body. It finished the lulling of her senses. She lay still, and the milk now being spooned into her mouth dribbled out again and on to the rug.

In the cottage the woman rose and stood beside her husband.

'D'ye think it's dying, Dan? It doesn't swallow any more.'

'I don't know, Dally. It may live the night. We've done the best we can. All we can do is just – let it be.'

The woman stared at it.

'Dan, I think I'll sit up wi' it.'

'Now, Dally. Ye've done your best, and . . .'

'But it might need some help and . . . it's such a bonnie dog, Dan.'

'Bonnie! That ugly mongrel of a stray . . .'

'Oh, Dan. It's the bonniest dog I ever saw.'

Firmly the old woman planted herself in the rocking chair and settled herself for a night of watching.

A week later Mrs Fadden sat in her chair. The morning sunlight streamed through the window, and the memory of the storm seemed like a dream of long ago. She looked over her glasses and beamed at Lassie, lying on the rug, her ears erect.

'It's himself,' she said aloud. 'And you know it, don't you?'

There came the footsteps of her husband, and then he door opened.

'Ye know, Dan, she knows your footsteps already,' the woman said proudly.

'Ah,' he said sceptically.

'She does,' Dally maintained. 'The other day, when that pedlar came, she just raised the roof, I'll tell you. My word, she let him know someone was home while you were in town! But she doesn't make a sound when she hears you coming – so she must know your foot- steps.'

'Ah,' the man replied again.

'She's smart – and she's bonnie,' the woman said – more to the dog than to the man. 'Isn't she bonnie, Dan?'

'Aye, that she is.'

'And first off you said she was ugly.'

'Aye, but that was before . . .'

'See, I just took an old comb and did her coat all pretty.'

They looked at Lassie, now lying with head erect in that lion-like posture that collies so often take. Her slim muzzle was held gracefully above the ruff that once again was beginning to show glossy white.

'Doesn't she look different?' the woman asked proudly.

'Aye, that's it, Dally,' the man said dolefully.

The woman caught his ominous tone.

'Well, what's the matter?'

'Eigh, Dally. Ye see, that's just it. First off, I thought she was a mongrel. But now . . . well, she's a fine dog.'

'Of course she's a fine dog,' the old woman said happily. 'All she needed was a bit of warmth and a little to eat and somebody to be kind to her.'

The man shook his head as if exasperated at his wife

who did not see what he was driving at.

'Aye, but don't ye understand, Dally? She's a fine dog – and now she's all cleaned up and getting better, ye can see she's a very valuable dog. And . . .'

'And what?'

'Well, a valuable dog will have owners somewhere.'

'Owners? Fine owners who'd leave a puir thing oot wandering and bony and starving on a night like we took her in. Owners, indeed!'

The man shook his head and sat in his chair heavily. He stuffed his clay pipe.

'No, Dally, it's no good. She's a valuable dog, and I can see it now. So don't get your heart set on her, because any day the owner might come . . .'

The woman sat, her mind worrying over this new and terrible thought. Her beautiful dog – *her* dog! She stared at the fire and then, for a long time, at Lassie. Finally she spoke: 'Well, then, if this has got to be taken away fro' us, Dan – it might as well be sooner as later. Oh, if anyone owns it! Find out, will ye, Dan? Go ask around.'

The man nodded.

'It's honest,' he said. 'I'll go to town and ask around tomorrow.'

'No, Dan, today. Go right now. For I'd never have a minute's peace nor sleep a wink till I knew. Go today and ask around everywhere, and then if she's to go, she'll go. And if nobody owns her, then we've done our duty and can rest easy.'

The man puffed his pipe, but the woman gave him no rest until he agreed to go that day.

At noon he set out, walking slowly down the road to the town four miles away. All through the afternoon the woman rocked. Sometimes she went to the door and looked down the highway.

It was a long afternoon. The minutes dragged for the old woman. It was falling dusk when at last she heard the footsteps. Almost before the door opened she began:

'Well?'

'I asked all aroond the place – everywhere – and nobody seems to ha' lost her.'

'Then she's ours!'

The woman beamed with joy and looked at the proud dog, still thin and pinched, but to her the perfection of canine breeding.

'She's ours,' she repeated. 'We gave them their chance. Now she's ours.'

'Well, now, Dally. They might pass by chance and see her, so don't . . .'

'She's ours now,' the woman repeated stolidly.

Mentally she was resolving that no owner should pass and ever see the dog. She would see to that. The dog should stay always beside her in the cottage. She would not have it running around loose outside for that terrible, unknown owner to see as he passed by!

Like Summer Tempests Came His Tears

from *The Wind in the Willows*
by Kenneth Grahame

THE Rat put out a neat little brown paw, gripped Toad firmly by the scruff of the neck, and gave a great hoist and a pull and the waterlogged Toad came up slowly but surely over the edge of the hole, till at last he stood safe and sound in the hall, streaked with mud and weed to be sure, and with the water streaming off him, but happy and high-spirited as of old, now that he found himself once more in the house of a friend, and dodgings and evasions were over, and he could lay aside a disguise that was unworthy of his position and wanted such a lot of living up to.

'Oh, Ratty!' he cried. 'I've been through such times since I saw you last, you can't think! Such trials, such sufferings, and all so nobly borne! Then such escapes, such disguises, such subterfuges, and all so cleverly planned and carried out! Been in prison – got out of it, of course! Been thrown into a canal – swam ashore! Stole a horse – sold him for a large sum of money! Humbugged everybody – made 'em all do exactly what I wanted! Oh, I *am* a smart Toad, and no mistake!

What do you think my last exploit was? Just hold on till I tell you –'

'Toad,' said the Water Rat, gravely and firmly, 'you go off upstairs at once, and take off the old cotton rag that looks as if it might formerly have belonged to some washerwoman, and clean yourself thoroughly, and put on some of my clothes and try and come down looking like a gentleman if you *can*; for a more shabby, bedraggled, disreputable-looking object than you are I never set eyes on in my whole life! Now, stop swaggering and arguing, and be off! I'll have something to say to you later!'

Toad was at first inclined to stop and do some talking back at him. He had had enough of being ordered about when he was in prison, and here was the thing being begun all over again, apparently; and by a Rat, too! However, he caught sight of himself in the looking glass over the hatstand, with the rusty black bonnet perched rakishly over one eye, and he changed his mind and went very quickly and humbly upstairs to the Rat's dressing room. There he had a thorough wash and brush-up, changed his clothes, and stood for a long time before the glass, contemplating himself with pride and pleasure, and thinking what utter idiots all the people must have been to have ever mistaken him for one moment for a washerwoman.

By the time he came down again luncheon was on the table, and very glad Toad was to see it, for he had been through some trying experiences and had taken much hard exercise since the excellent breakfast provided for him by the gypsy. While they ate Toad told the Rat all his adventures, dwelling chiefly on his own cleverness, and presence of mind in emergencies, and cunning in tight places; and rather making out that he had been having a gay and highly coloured experience. But the more he talked and boasted, the more grave and silent the Rat became.

When at last Toad had talked himself to a standstill, there was silence for a while; and then the Rat said, 'Now, Toady, I don't want to give you pain, after all you've been through already; but seriously don't you see what an awful ass you've been making of yourself? On your own admission you have been handcuffed, imprisoned, starved, chased, terrified out of your life, insulted, jeered at, and ignominiously flung into the water – by a woman, too! Where's the amusement in that? Where does the fun come in? And all because you must needs go and steal a motorcar. You know that you've never had anything but trouble from motorcars from the moment you first set eyes on one. But if you *will* be mixed up with them – as you generally are, five minutes after you've started – why *steal* them? Be a cripple, if you think it's exciting; be a bankrupt, for a change, if you've set your mind on it; but why choose to be a convict? When are you going to be sensible, and think of your friends, and try and be a credit to them? Do you suppose it's any pleasure for me, for instance, to hear animals saying, as I go about, that I'm the chap that keeps company with jailbirds?'

Now, it was a very comforting point in Toad's character that he was a thoroughly goodhearted animal, and never minded being jawed by those who were his real friends. And even when most set upon a thing, he was always able to see the other side of the question. So although, while the Rat was talking so seriously, he kept saying to himself mutinously, 'But it *was* fun, though! Awful fun!' and making strange suppressed noises inside him, k-i-ck-ck-ck-ck, and poop-p-p, and other sounds resembling stifled snorts, or the opening of sodawater bottles, yet when the Rat had quite finished, he heaved a deep sigh and said, very nicely and humbly, 'Quite right, Ratty! How *sound* you always are! Yes, I've been a conceited old ass, I can quite see that; but now I'm going to be a good Toad, and not do it any more. As for motorcars, I've not been at all so keen about them since my last ducking in that river of yours. The fact is, while I was hanging on to the edge of your hole and getting my breath, I had a sudden idea – a really brilliant idea – connected with motorboats – there, there! don't take on so, old chap, and stamp, and upset things; it was only an idea, and we won't talk any more about it now. We'll have our coffee, *and* a smoke, and a quiet chat, and then I'm going to stroll gently down to Toad Hall, and get into clothes of my own, and set things going again on the old lines. I've had enough of adventures. I shall lead a quiet, steady, respectable life, pottering about my property, and improving it, and doing a little landscape gardening at times. There will always be a bit of dinner for my friends when they come to see me; and I shall keep a pony-chaise to jog about the country in, just as I used to in the good old days, before I got restless, and wanted to *do* things.'

'Stroll gently down to Toad Hall?' cried the Rat, greatly excited. 'What are you talking about? Do you mean to say you haven't *heard*?'

'Heard what?' said Toad, turning rather pale. 'Go on, Ratty! Quick! Don't spare me! What haven't I heard?'

'Do you mean to tell me,' shouted the Rat, thumping with his little fist upon the table, 'that you've heard nothing about the Stoats and Weasels?'

'What, the Wild Wooders?' cried Toad, trembling in every limb. 'No, not a word! What have they been doing?'

'– And how they've been and taken Toad Hall?' continued the Rat.

Toad leaned his elbows on the table, and his chin on his paws; and a large tear welled up in each of his eyes, overflowed and splashed on the table, plop! plop!

'Go on, Ratty,' he murmured presently, 'tell me all. The worst is over. I am an animal again. I can bear it.'

'When you – got – into that – that – trouble of

yours,' said the Rat slowly and impressively, 'I mean, when you – disappeared from society for a time, over that misunderstanding about a – a machine, you know –'

Toad merely nodded.

'Well, it was a good deal talked about down here, naturally,' continued the Rat, 'not only along the river-side, but even in the Wild Wood. Animals took sides, as always happens. The River-bankers stuck up for you, and said you had been infamously treated, and there was no justice to be had in the land nowadays. But the Wild Wood animals said hard things, and served you right, and it was time this sort of thing was stopped. And they got very cocky, and went about saying you were done for this time! You would never come back again, never, never!'

Toad nodded once more, keeping silence.

'That's the sort of little beasts they are,' the Rat went on. 'But Mole and Badger, they stuck out, through thick and thin, that you would come back again soon, some-how. They didn't know exactly how, but somehow!'

Toad began to sit up in his chair again, and to smirk a little.

'They argued from history,' continued the Rat. 'They said that no criminal laws had ever been known to prevail against cheek and plausibility such as yours, combined with the power of a long purse. So they arranged to move their things into Toad Hall, and sleep there, and keep it aired, and have it all ready for you when you turned up. They didn't guess what was going to happen, of course; still, they had their suspicions of the Wild Wood animals. Now I come to the most painful and tragic part of my story. One dark night – it was a *very* dark night, and blowing hard, too, and raining simply cats and dogs – a band of weasels, armed to the teeth, crept silently up the carriage drive to the front entrance. Simultaneously, a body of desperate ferrets, advancing through the kitchen garden, possessed themselves of the backyard and offices; while a company of skirmishing stoats who stuck at nothing occupied the conservatory and the billiard room, and held the French windows opening onto the lawn.

'The Mole and the Badger were sitting by the fire in the smoking room, telling stories and suspected nothing, for it wasn't a night for any animals to be out in, when those bloodthirsty villains broke down the doors and rushed in upon them from every side. They made the best fight they could, but what was the good? They were unarmed, and taken by surprise, and what can two animals do against hundreds? They took and beat them severely with sticks, those two poor faithful creatures, and turned them out into the cold and the wet, with many insulting and uncalled-for remarks!'

Here the unfeeling Toad broke into a snigger, and then pulled himself together and tried to look particularly solemn.

'And the Wild Wooders have been living in Toad Hall ever since,' continued the Rat; 'and going on simply anyhow! Lying in bed half the day, and breakfast at all hours, and the place in such a mess (I'm told) it's not fit to be seen! Eating your grub, and drinking your drink, and making bad jokes about you, and singing vulgar songs, about – well, about prisons, and magistrates, and policemen; horrid personal songs, with no humour in them. And they're telling the tradespeople and everybody that they've come to stay for good.'

'Oh, have they!' said Toad, getting up and seizing a stick. 'I'll jolly soon see about that!'

'It's no good, Toad!' called the Rat after him. 'You'd better come back and sit down; you'll only get into trouble.'

But the Toad was off, and there was no holding him. He marched rapidly down the road, his stick over his shoulder, fuming and muttering to himself in his anger, till he got near his front gate, when suddenly there popped up from behind the palings a long yellow ferret with a gun.

'Who comes there?' said the ferret sharply.

'Stuff and nonsense!' said Toad very angrily. 'What do you mean by talking like that to me? Come out of it at once, or I'll –'

The ferret said never a word, but he brought his gun up to his shoulder. Toad prudently dropped flat in the road, and *Bang*! a bullet whistled over his head.

The startled Toad scrambled to his feet and scampered off down the road as hard as he could; and as he ran he heard the ferret laughing, and other horrid thin little laughs taking it up and carrying on the sound.

He went back, very crestfallen, and told the Water Rat.

'What did I tell you?' said the Rat. 'It's no good. They've got sentries posted, and they are all armed. You must just wait.'

Still, Toad was not inclined to give in all at once. So he got out the boat, and set off rowing up the river to where the garden front of Toad Hall came down to the waterside.

Arriving within sight of his old home, he rested on his oars and surveyed the land cautiously. All seemed very peaceful and deserted and quiet. He could see the whole front of Toad Hall, glowing in the evening sunshine, the pigeons settling by twos and threes along the straight line of the roof; the garden, a blaze of flowers; the creek that led up to the boathouse, the little wooden bridge that crossed it; all tranquil, uninhabited, apparently waiting for his return. He would try the boathouse first, he thought. Very warily he paddled up to the mouth of the creek, and was just passing under the bridge, when . . . *Crash*!

A great stone, dropped from above, smashed through the bottom of the boat. It filled and sank, and Toad found himself struggling in deep water. Looking up, he saw two stoats leaning over the parapet of the bridge and watching him with great glee. 'It will be your head next time, Toady!' they called out to him. The indignant Toad swam to shore, while the stoats laughed and laughed, supporting each other, and laughed again, till they nearly had two fits – that is, one fit each, of course.

The Toad retraced his weary way on foot, and related his disappointing experiences to the Water Rat once more.

'Well, *what* did I tell you?' said the Rat very crossly. 'And, now, look here! See what you've been and done! Lost me my boat that I was so fond of, that's what you've done! And simply ruined that nice suit of clothes that I lent you! Really, Toad, of all the trying animals – I wonder you manage to keep any friends at all!'

The Toad saw at once how wrongly and foolishly he had acted. He admitted his errors and wrongheadedness and made a full apology to Rat for losing his boat and spoiling his clothes. And he wound up by saying, with that frank self-surrender which always disarmed his friends' criticism and won them back to his side, 'Ratty! I see that I have been a headstrong and a wilful Toad! Henceforth, believe me, I will be humble and submissive, and will take no action without your kind advice and full approval!'

'If that is really so,' said the good-natured Rat, already appeased, 'then my advice to you is, considering the lateness of the hour, to sit down and have your supper, which will be on the table in a minute, and be very patient. For I am convinced that we can do nothing until we have seen the Mole and the Badger, and heard their latest news, and held conference and taken their advice in this difficult matter.'

'Oh, ah, yes, of course, the Mole and the Badger,' said Toad lightly. 'What's become of them, the dear fellows? I had forgotten all about them.'

'Well may you ask!' said the Rat reproachfully. 'While you were riding about the country in expensive motor-cars, and galloping proudly on blood horses, and break-fasting on the fat of the land, those two poor devoted animals have been camping out in the open, in every sort of weather, living very rough by day and lying very hard by night watching over your house, patrolling your boundaries, keeping a constant eye on the stoats and the weasels, scheming and planning and contriving how to get your property back for you. You don't deserve to have such true and loyal friends, Toad, you don't, really. Some day, when it's too late, you'll be sorry you didn't value them more while you had them!'

'I'm an ungrateful beast, I know,' sobbed Toad, shedding bitter tears. 'Let me go out and find them, out into the cold, dark night, and share their hardships, and try and prove by – Hold on a bit! Surely I heard the chink of dishes on a tray! Supper's here at last, hooray! Come on, Ratty!'

The Rat remembered that poor Toad had been on prison fare for a considerable time, and that large allowances had therefore to be made. He followed him to the table accordingly, and hospitably encouraged him in his gallant efforts to make up for past privations.

They had just finished their meal and resumed their armchairs, when there came a heavy knock at the door.

Toad was nervous, but the Rat, nodding mysteriously at him, went straight up to the door and opened it, and in walked Mr. Badger.

He had all the appearance of one who for some nights had been kept away from home and all its little comforts and conveniences. His shoes were covered with mud, and he was looking very rough and tousled; but then he had never been a very smart man, the Badger, at the best of times. He came solemnly up to Toad, shook him by the paw, and said, 'Welcome home, Toad! Alas! what am I saying? Home, indeed! This is a poor homecoming.

*He came solemnly up to Toad, shook him by the paw, and said,
'Welcome home, Toad!'*

Unhappy Toad!' Then he turned his back on him, sat
down to the table, drew his chair up, and helped himself
to a large slice of cold pie.

Toad was quite alarmed at this very serious and
portentous style of greeting but the Rat whispered to
him, 'Never mind; don't take any notice; and don't say
anything to him just yet. He's always rather low and
despondent when he's wanting his victuals. In half an
hour's time he'll be quite a different animal.'

So they waited in silence, and presently there came
another and a lighter knock. The Rat, with a nod to
Toad, went to the door and ushered in the Mole, very
shabby and unwashed, with bits of hay and straw stick-
ing in his fur.

'Hooray! Here's old Toad!' cried the Mole, his face
beaming. 'Fancy having you back again!' And he began

to dance round him. 'We never dreamed you would turn up so soon! Why, you must have managed to escape, you clever, ingenious, intelligent Toad!'

The Rat, alarmed, pulled him by the elbow; but it was too late. Toad was puffing and swelling already.

'Clever? Oh, no!' he said. 'I'm not really clever, according to my friends. I've only broken out of the strongest prison in England, that's all! And captured a railway train and escaped on it, that's all! And disguised myself and gone about the country humbugging every-body, that's all! Oh, no! I'm a stupid ass, I am! I'll tell you one or two of my little adventures, Mole, and you shall judge for yourself!'

'Well, well,' said the Mole, moving towards the supper table; 'supposing you talk while I eat. Not a bite since breakfast! Oh my! Oh my!' And he sat down and helped himself liberally to cold beef and pickles.

Toad straddled on the hearthrug, thrust his paw into his trouser pocket and pulled out a handful of silver. 'Look at that!' he cried, displaying it. 'That's not so bad, is it, for a few minutes' work? And how do you think I done it, Mole? Horse dealing! That's how I done it!'

'Go on, Toad,' said the Mole, immensely interested.

'Toad, do be quiet, please!' said the Rat. 'And don't you egg him on, Mole, when you know what he is; but please tell us as soon as possible what the position is, and what's best to be done, now that Toad is back at last.'

'The position's about as bad as it can be,' replied the Mole grumpily, 'and as for what's to be done, why, blest if I know! The Badger and I have been round and round the place, by night and by day; always the same thing. Sentries posted everywhere, guns poked out at us, stones thrown at us; always an animal on the lookout, and when they see us, my! how they do laugh! That's what annoys me most!'

'It's a very difficult situation,' said the Rat, reflecting deeply. 'But I think I see now, in the depths of my mind, what Toad really ought to do. I will tell you. He ought to –'

'No, he oughtn't!' shouted the Mole, with his mouth full. 'Nothing of the sort! You don't understand. What he ought to do is, he ought to –'

'Well, I shan't do it, anyway!' cried Toad, getting excited. 'I'm not going to be ordered about by you fellows! It's my house we're talking about, and I know exactly what to do, and I'll tell you. I'm going to –'

By this time they were all three talking at once, at the top of their voices, and the noise was simply deafening, when a thin, dry voice made itself heard, saying, 'Be quiet at once, all of you!' and instantly everyone was silent.

It was the Badger, who, having finished his pie, had turned round in his chair and was looking at them severely. When he saw that he had secured their attention, and that they were evidently waiting for him to address them, he turned back to the table again and reached out for the cheese. And so great was the respect commanded by the solid qualities of that admirable animal, that not another word was uttered until he had quite finished his repast and brushed the crumbs from his knees. The Toad fidgeted a good deal, but the Rat held him firmly down.

When the Badger had quite done, he got up from his seat and stood before the fireplace, reflecting deeply. At last he spoke.

'Toad!' he said severely. 'You bad, troublesome little animal! Aren't you ashamed of yourself? What do you think your father, my old friend, would have said if he had been here tonight, and had known of all your goings on?'

Toad, who was on the sofa by this time, with his legs up, rolled over on his face, shaken by sobs of contrition.

'There, there!' went on the Badger more kindly. 'Never mind. Stop crying. We're going to let bygones be bygones, and try and turn over a new leaf. But what the

Mole says is quite true. The stoats are on guard, at every point, and they make the best sentinels in the world. It's quite useless to think of attacking the place. They're too strong for us.'

'Then it's all over,' sobbed the Toad, crying into the sofa cushions. 'I shall go and enlist for a soldier, and never see my dear Toad Hall any more!'

'Come, cheer up, Toady!' said the Badger. 'There are more ways of getting back a place than taking it by storm. I haven't said my last word yet. Now I'm going to tell you a great secret.'

Toad sat up slowly and dried his eyes. Secrets had an immense attraction for him, because he never could keep one, and he enjoyed the sort of unhallowed thrill he experienced when he went and told another animal, after having faithfully promised not to.

'There – is – an – underground – passage,' said the Badger impressively, 'that leads from the river bank, quite near here right up into the middle of Toad Hall.'

'Oh, nonsense, Badger!' said Toad rather airily. 'You've been listening to some of the yarns they spin in the public houses about here. I know every inch of Toad Hall, inside and out. Nothing of the sort, I do assure you!'

'My young friend,' said the Badger with great severity, 'your father, who was a worthy animal – a lot worthier than some others I know – was a particular friend of mine, and told me a great deal he wouldn't have dreamed of telling you. He discovered that passage – he didn't make it, of course; that was done hundreds of years before he ever came to live there – and he repaired it and cleaned it out, because he thought it might come in useful some day, in case of trouble or danger; and he showed it to me. "Don't let my son know about it," he said. "He's a good boy, but very light and volatile in character, and simply cannot hold his tongue. If he's ever in a real fix, and it would be of use to him, you may tell him about the secret passage; but not before." '

The other animals looked hard at Toad to see how he would take it. Toad was inclined to be sulky at first but he brightened up immediately, like the good fellow he was.

'Well, well,' he said, 'perhaps I am a bit of a talker. A popular fellow such as I am – my friends get round me – we chaff, we sparkle, we tell witty stories – and somehow my tongue gets wagging. I have the gift of conversation. I've been told I ought to have a *salon*, whatever that may be. Never mind. Go on, Badger. How's this passage of yours going to help us?'

'I've found out a thing or two lately,' continued the Badger. 'I got Otter to disguise himself as a sweep and call at the back door with brushes over his shoulder, asking for a job. There's going to be a big banquet tomorrow night. It's somebody's birthday – the Chief Weasel's, I believe – and all the weasels will be gathered together in the dining hall, eating and drinking and laughing and carrying on, suspecting nothing. No guns, no swords, no sticks, no arms of any sort whatever!'

'But the sentinels will be posted as usual,' remarked the Rat.

'Exactly,' said the Badger; 'that is my point. The weasels will trust entirely to their excellent sentinels. And that is where the passage comes in. That very useful tunnel leads right up under the butler's pantry, next to the dining hall!'

'Aha! that squeaky board in the butler's pantry!' said Toad. 'Now I understand it!'

'We shall creep out quietly into the butler's pantry –' cried the Mole.

'– with our pistols and swords and sticks –' shouted the Rat.

'– and rush in upon them,' said the Badger.

'– and whack 'em, and whack 'em, and whack 'em!'

cried the Toad in ecstasy, running round and round the room, and jumping over the chairs.

'Very well, then,' said the Badger, resuming his usual dry manner, 'our plan is settled, and there's nothing more for you to argue and squabble about. So, as it's getting very late, all of you go right off to bed at once. We will make all the necessary arrangements in the course of the morning tomorrow.'

Toad, of course, went off to bed dutifully with the rest – he knew better than to refuse – though he was feeling much too excited to sleep. But he had had a long day, with many events crowded into it; and sheets and blankets were very friendly and comforting things, after plain straw, and not too much of it, spread on the stone floor of a drafty cell; and his head had not been many seconds on his pillow before he was snoring happily. Naturally, he dreamed a good deal; about roads that ran away from him just when he wanted them, and canals that chased him and caught him, and a barge that sailed into the banqueting hall with his week's washing, just as he was giving a dinner party; and he was alone in the secret passage, pushing onwards, but it twisted and turned round and shook itself, and sat up on its end; yet somehow, at the last, he found himself back in Toad Hall, safe and triumphant, with all his friends gathered round about him, earnestly assuring him that he really was a clever Toad.

He slept till a late hour next morning, and by the time he got down he found that the other animals had finished their breakfast some time before. The Mole had slipped off somewhere by himself, without telling any-one where he was going. The Badger sat in the arm-chair, reading the paper, and not concerning himself in the slightest about what was going to happen that very evening. The Rat, on the other hand, was running round the room busily, with his arms full of weapons of every kind, distributing them in four little heaps on the floor, and saying excitedly under his breath, as he ran, 'Here's-a-sword-for-the-Rat, here's-a-sword-for-the-Mole, here's-a-sword-for-the-Toad, here's-a-sword-for-the-Badger! Here's-a-pistol-for-the-Rat, here's-a-pistol-for-the-Mole, here's-a-pistol-for-the-Toad, here's-a-pistol-for-the-Badger!' And so on, in a regular, rhythmical way, while the four little heaps gradually grew and grew.

'That's all very well, Rat,' said the Badger presently, looking at the busy little animal over the edge of his newspaper; 'I'm not blaming you. But just let us once get past the stoats, with those detestable guns of theirs, and I assure you we shan't want any swords or pistols. We four, with our sticks, once we're inside the dining hall, why, we shall clear the floor of all the lot of them in five minutes. I'd have done the whole thing by myself, only I didn't want to deprive you fellows of the fun!'

'It's as well to be on the safe side,' said the Rat reflectively, polishing a pistol-barrel on his sleeve and looking along it.

The Toad, having finished his breakfast, picked up a stout stick and swung it vigorously, belabouring imaginary animals. 'I'll learn 'em to steal my house!' he cried. 'I'll learn 'em, I'll learn 'em!'

'Don't say "learn 'em," Toad,' said the Rat, greatly shocked. 'It's not good English.'

'What are you always nagging at Toad for?' inquired the Badger rather peevishly. 'What's the matter with his English? It's the same what I use myself, and if it's good enough for me, it ought to be good enough for you!'

'I'm very sorry,' said the Rat humbly. 'Only I *think* it ought to be "teach 'em" not "learn 'em." '

'But we don't *want* to teach 'em,' replied the Badger. 'We want to *learn* 'em – learn 'em, learn 'em! And what's more, we're going to *do* it, too!'

'Oh, very well, have it your own way,' said the Rat. He was getting rather muddled about it himself, and presently he retired into a corner, where he could be heard muttering, 'Learn 'em, teach 'em, teach 'em, learn 'em!' till the Badger told him rather sharply to leave off.

Presently the Mole came tumbling into the room, evidently very pleased with himself. 'I've been having such fun!' he began at once; 'I've been getting a rise out of the stoats!'

'I hope you've been very careful, Mole?' said the Rat anxiously.

'I should hope so, too,' said the Mole confidently. 'I got the idea when I went into the kitchen, to see about Toad's breakfast being kept hot for him. I found that old washerwoman dress that he came home in yesterday hanging out on a towel-horse before the fire. So I put it on, and the bonnet as well, and the shawl, and off I went to Toad Hall, as bold as you please. The sentries were on the lookout, of course, with their guns and their "Who comes there?" and all the rest of their nonsense. "Good morning, gentlemen!" says I, very respectful. "Want any washing done today?" '

'They looked at me very proud and stiff and haughty, and said, "Go away, washerwoman! We don't do any washing on duty." "Or any other time?" says I. Ho, ho, ho! Wasn't I *funny*, Toad?'

'Poor frivolous animal!' said Toad very loftily. The fact is, he felt exceeding jealous of Mole for what he had just done. It was exactly what he would have liked to have done himself, if only he had thought of it first, and hadn't gone and overslept himself.

'Some of the stoats turned quite pink,' continued the Mole, 'and the sergeant in charge, he said to me, very short, he said, "Now run away, my good woman, run away! Don't keep my men idling and talking on their posts." "Run away?" says I; "it won't be me that'll be running away, in a very short time from now!" '

'Oh, *Moly*, how could you?' said the Rat, dismayed.

The Badger laid down his paper.

'I could see them pricking up their ears and looking at each other,' went on the Mole, 'and the sergeant said to them, "Never mind *her*; she doesn't know what she's talking about." '

' "Oh, don't I?" said I. "Well, let me tell you this. My daughter, she washes for Mr. Badger, and that'll show you whether I know what I'm talking about; and *you'll* know pretty soon, too! A hundred bloodthirsty Badgers, armed with rifles, are going to attack Toad Hall this very night, by way of the paddock. Six boatloads of Rats, with pistols and cutlasses, will come up the river and effect a landing in the garden; while a picked body of Toads, known as the Die-hards, or the Death-or-Glory Toads, will storm the orchard and carry everything before them, yelling for vengeance. There won't be much left of you to wash, by the time they've done with you, unless you clear out while you have the chance!" Then I ran away, and when I was out of sight I hid; and presently I came creeping back along the ditch and took a peep at them through the hedge. They were all as nervous and flustered as could be, running all ways at once, and falling over each other, and everyone giving orders to everybody else and not listening; and the sergeant kept sending off parties of stoats to distant parts of the grounds, and then sending other fellows to fetch 'em back again; and I heard them saying to each other, "That's *just* like the weasels; they're to stop comfortably in the banqueting hall, and have feasting and toasts and songs and all sorts of fun, while we must stay on guard in the cold and the dark, and in the end be cut to pieces by bloodthirsty Badgers!" '

'Oh, you silly ass, Mole!' cried the Toad. 'You've been and spoiled everything!'

'Mole,' said the Badger, in his dry, quiet way, 'I perceive you have more sense in your little finger than some other animals have in the whole of their fat bodies. You have managed excellently, and I begin to have great hopes of you. Good Mole! Clever Mole!'

The Toad was simply wild with jealousy, more especially as he couldn't make out for the life of him what the Mole had done that was so particularly clever; but, fortunately for him, before he could show temper or expose himself to the Badger's sarcasm, the bell rang for luncheon.

It was a simple but sustaining meal – bacon and broad beans, and a macaroni pudding; and when they had quite done, the Badger settled himself into an armchair, and said, 'Well, we've got our work cut out for us tonight, and it will probably be pretty late before we're quite through with it; so I'm just going to take forty winks, while I can.' And he drew a handkerchief over his face and was soon snoring.

The anxious and laborious Rat at once resumed his preparations, and started running between his four little heaps, muttering, 'Here's-a-belt-for-the Rat, here's-a-belt-for-the-Mole, here's-a-belt-for-the-Toad, here's-a-belt-for-the-Badger!' and so on, with every fresh accoutrement he produced, to which there seemed really no end; so the Mole drew his arm through Toad's, led him out into the open air, shoved him into a wicker chair, and made him tell him all his adventures from beginning to end, which Toad was only too willing to do. The Mole was a good listener, and Toad, with no one to check his statements or to criticize in an unfriendly spirit, rather let himself go. Indeed, much that he related belonged more properly to the category of what-might-have-happened-had-I-only-thought-of-it-in-time-instead-of-ten-minutes-afterwards. Those are always the best and the raciest adventures; and why should they not be truly ours, as much as the somewhat inadequate things that really come off?

The Cowardly Lion

from *The Marvellous Land of Oz*
by L. Frank Baum

ALL this time Dorothy and her companions had been walking through the thick woods. The road was still paved with yellow brick, but these were much covered by dried branches and dead leaves from the trees, and the walking was not at all good.

There were few birds in this part of the forest, for birds love the open country where there is plenty of sunshine; but now and then there came a deep growl from some wild animal hidden among the trees. These sounds made the little girl's heart beat fast, for she did not know what made them; but Toto knew, and he walked close to Dorothy's side, and did not even bark in return.

'How long will it be,' the child asked of the Tin Woodman, 'before we are out of the forest?'

'I cannot tell,' was the answer, 'for I have never been to the Emerald City. But my father went there once, when I was a boy, and he said it was a long journey through a dangerous country, although nearer. to the city were Oz dwells the country is beautiful. But I am not afraid so long as I have my oil-can, and nothing can hurt the Scarecrow, while you bear upon your forehead the mark of the good Witch's kiss, and that will protect you from harm.'

'But Toto!' said the girl; 'what will protect him?'

'We must protect him ourselves, if he is in danger,' replied the Tin Woodman.

Just as he spoke there came from the forest a terrible roar, and the next moment a great Lion bounded into the road. With one blow of his paw he sent the Scarecrow spinning over and over to the edge of the road, and then he struck at the Tin Woodman with his sharp claws. But, to the Lion's surprise, he could make no impression on the tin, although the Woodman fell over in the road and lay still.

Little Toto, now that he had an enemy to face, ran barking toward the Lion, and the great beast had opened his mouth to bite the dog, when Dorothy, fearing Toto would be killed, and heedless of danger, rushed forward and slapped the Lion upon his nose as hard as she could, while she cried out:

'Don't you dare to bite Toto! You ought to be ashamed of yourself, a big beast like you, to bite a poor little dog!'

'I didn't bite him,' said the Lion, as he rubbed his nose with his paw where Dorothy had hit it.

'No, but you tried to,' she retorted. 'You are nothing but a big coward.'

'I know it,' said the Lion, hanging his head in shame; I've always known it. But how can I help it?'

'I don't know, I'm sure. To think of your striking a stuffed man, like the poor Scarecrow!'

'Is he stuffed?' asked the Lion, in surprise, as he watched her pick up the Scarecrow and set him upon his feet, while she patted him into shape again.

'Of course he's stuffed,' replied Dorothy, who was still angry.

'That's why he went over so easily,' remarked the Lion. 'It astonished me to see him whirl around so. Is the other one stuffed, also?'

'No,' said Dorothy, 'he's made of tin.' And she helped the Woodman up again.

'That's why he nearly blunted my claws,' said the Lion. 'When they scratched against the tin it made a cold shiver run down my back. What is that little animal you are so tender of?'

'He is my dog, Toto,' answered Dorothy.

'Is he made of tin, or stuffed?' asked the Lion.

'Neither. He's a – a – a meat dog,' said the girl.

'Oh! He's a curious animal, and seems remarkably small, now that I look at him. No one would think of biting such a little thing except a coward like me,' continued the Lion, sadly.

'What makes you a coward?' asked Dorothy, looking at the great beast in wonder, for he was as big as a small horse.

'It's a mystery,' replied the Lion. 'I suppose I was born that way. All the other animals in the forest naturally expect me to be brave, for the Lion is everywhere thought to be the King of Beasts. I learned that if I roared very loudly every living thing was frightened and got out of my way. Whenever I've met a man I've been awfully scared; but I just roared at him, and he has always run away as fast as he could go. If the elephants and the tigers and the bears had ever tried to fight me, I should have run myself – I'm such a coward; but just as soon as they hear me roar they all try to get away from me, and of course I let them go.'

'But that isn't right. The King of Beasts shouldn't be a coward,' said the Scarecrow.

'I know it,' returned the Lion, wiping a tear from his eye with the tip of his tail; 'it is my great sorrow, and makes my life very unhappy. But whenever there is danger my heart begins to beat fast.'

'Perhaps you have heart disease,' said the Tin Wood-man.

'It may be,' said the Lion.

'If you have,' continued the Tin Woodman, 'you ought to be glad, for it proves you have a heart. For my part, I have no heart so I cannot have heart disease.'

'Perhaps,' said the Lion, thoughtfully, 'if I had no heart I should not be a coward.'

'Have you brains?' asked the Scarecrow.

'I suppose so. I've never looked to see,' replied the Lion.

'I am going to the Great Oz to ask him to give me some,' remarked the Scarecrow, 'for my head is stuffed with straw.'

'And I am going to ask him to give me a heart,' said the Woodman.

'And I am going to ask him to send Toto and me back to Kansas,' added Dorothy.

'Do you think Oz could give me courage?' asked the Cowardly Lion.

'Just as easily as he could give me brains,' said the Scarecrow.

'Or give me a heart,' said the Tin Woodman.

'Or send me back to Kansas,' said Dorothy.

'Then, if you don't mind, I'll go with you,' said the Lion, 'for my life is simply unbearable without a bit of courage.'

'You will be very welcome,' answered Dorothy, 'for you will help to keep away the other wild beasts. It seems to me they must be more cowardly than you are if they allow you to scare them so easily.'

'They really are,' said the Lion; 'but that doesn't make me any braver, and as long as I know myself to be a coward I shall be unhappy.'

So once more the little company set off upon the journey, the Lion walking with stately strides at Dorothy's side. Toto did not approve this new comrade at first, for he could not forget how nearly he had been crushed between the Lion's great jaws; but after a time he became more at ease, and presently Toto and the Cowardly Lion had grown to be good friends.

During the rest of that day there was no other adventure to mar the peace of their journey. Once, indeed, the Tin Woodman stepped upon a beetle that was crawling along the road, and killed the poor little thing. This made the Tin Woodman very unhappy for he was

always careful not to hurt any living creature; and as he walked along he wept several tears of sorrow and regret. The tears ran slowly down his face and over the hinges of his jaw, and there they rusted. When Dorothy presently asked him a question the Tin Woodman could not open his mouth, for his jaws were tightly rusted together. He became greatly frightened at this and made many motions to Dorothy to relieve him, but she could not understand. The Lion was also puzzled to know what was wrong. But the Scarecrow seized the oil-can from Dorothy's basket and oiled the Woodman's jaws, so that after a few moments he could talk as well as before.

'This will serve me a lesson,' said he, 'to look where I step. For if I should kill another bug or beetle I should surely cry again, and crying rusts my jaws so that I cannot speak.'

Thereafter he walked very carefully, with his eyes on the road, and when he saw a tiny ant toiling by he would step over it, so as not to harm it. The Tin Woodman knew very well he had no heart, and therefore he took great care never to be cruel or unkind to anything.

'You people with hearts,' he said, 'have something to guide you, and need never do wrong; but I have no heart, and so I must be very careful. When Oz gives me a heart of course I needn't mind so much.'

A Happy Ending

from *Black Beauty* by Anna Sewell

I WAS sold to a corn dealer and baker whom Jerry knew, and with him he thought I should have good food and fair work. In the first he was quite right, and if my master had always been on the premises, I do not think I should have been overloaded. But there was a foreman who was always hurrying and driving everyone, and frequently when I had quite a full load, he would order something else to be taken on. My carter, whose name was Jakes, often said it was more than I ought to take, but the other always overruled him.

Jakes, like the other carters, always had the bearing rein up, which prevented me from drawing easily, and by the time I had been there three or four months, I found the work telling very much on my strength.

One day I was loaded more than usual, and part of the road was a steep uphill. I used all my strength, but I could not get on, and was obliged to stop. This did not please my driver, and he laid his whip on badly. 'Get on, lazy fellow,' he said, 'or I'll make you.'

Again I started the heavy load, and struggled on a few

yards. Again the whip came down, and again I struggled forward. The pain of that great cart whip was sharp, but my mind was hurt quite as much as my poor sides. To be punished and abused when I was doing my best was so hard it took the heart out of me.

A third time he was flogging me cruelly when a lady stepped quickly up to him and said in a sweet, earnest voice, 'Oh! Pray do not whip your horse any more. I am sure he is doing all he can, and the road is very steep! He is doing his best.'

'If doing his best won't get this load up, he must do something more than his best, that's all I know, ma'am,' said Jakes.

'But is it not a very heavy load?' she said.

'Yes, yes, too heavy,' he said. 'But that's not my fault. The foreman came just as we were starting, and would have three hundredweight more put on to save him trouble, and I must get on with it as well as I can.'

He was raising the whip again, when the lady said, 'Pray, stop. I think I can help you if you will let me.'

The man laughed.

'You see,' she said, 'you do not give him a fair chance. He cannot use all his power with his head held back as it is with that bearing rein. If you would take it off, I am sure he would do better – *do* try it,' she said. 'I should be very glad if you would.'

'Well, well,' said Jakes, with a short laugh. 'Anything to please a lady, of course. How far would you wish it down, ma'am?'

'Quite down. Give him his head altogether.'

The rein was taken off, and in a moment I put my head down to my very knees. What a comfort it was! Then I tossed it up and down several times to get the aching stiffness out of my neck.

'Poor fellow! That is what you wanted,' said she, patting and stroking me with her gentle hand. 'And now if you will speak kindly to him and lead him on, I believe he will be able to do better.'

Jakes took the rein. 'Come on, Blackie.'

I put down my head and threw my whole weight against the collar. I spared no strength. The load moved on, and I pulled it steadily up the hill, and then stopped to catch my breath.

The lady had walked along the footpath and now came across into the road. She stroked and patted my neck as I had not been patted for many a long day.

'You see he was quite willing when you gave him the chance. I am sure he is a fine-tempered creature, and I daresay he has known better days. You won't put that rein on him again, will you?' For he was just going to hitch it up on the old plan.

'Well ma'am, I can't deny that having his head has helped him up the hill, and I'll remember it another time, and thank you, ma'am. But if he went without a bearing rein I should be the laughing stock of all the carters. It is the fashion, you see.'

'Is it not better,' she said, 'to lead a good fashion, than to follow a bad one? A great many gentlemen do not use bearing reins now. My carriage horses have not worn them for fifteen years, and work with much less fatigue than those who have them. Besides,' she added in a very serious voice, 'we have no right to distress any of God's creatures without a very good reason. We call them dumb animals, and so they are, for they cannot tell us how they feel, but they do not suffer less because they have no words. But I must not detain you now. I thank you for trying my plan with your good horse, and I am sure you will find it far better than the whip. Good day.' With another soft pat on my neck, she stepped across the path and I saw her no more.

'That was a real lady, I'll be bound for it,' said Jakes to himself. 'She spoke just as polite as if I was a gentleman, and I'll try her plan, uphill, at any rate.' And I must do him the justice to say that he let my rein out several

The lady had walked along the footpath and now came across into the road

holes, and going uphill after that, he always gave me my head.

But the heavy loads went on. Good feed and fair rest will keep one's strength under full work, but no horse can stand against overloading. I was getting so thoroughly pulled down from this cause that a younger horse was bought in my place.

I may as well mention here what I suffered at this time from another cause. I had heard horses speak of it, but had never myself had experience of the evil. This was the badly lighted stable. There was only one small window at the end, and the consequence was that the stalls were almost dark. Besides the depressing effect this had on my spirits, it very much weakened my sight, and when I was suddenly brought out of the darkness into the glare of daylight, it was very painful to my eyes. Several times I stumbled over the threshold, and could scarcely see where I was going.

I believe, had I stayed there very long I should have become purblind, and that would have been a great misfortune. I have heard men say that a stone-blind horse was safer to drive than one which had imperfect sight, as it generally makes them very timid.

However, I escaped without any permanent injury to my sight, and was sold to a large cab owner.

I shall never forget my new master. He had black eyes and a hooked nose, a mouth as full of teeth as a bulldog's, and his voice was as harsh as the grinding of cart wheels over gravel stones. His name was Nicholas Skinner, and I believe he was the same man that poor Seedy Sam drove for.

I have heard men say that seeing is believing, but I should say that *feeling* is believing. Much as I had seen before, I never really knew till now the utter misery of a cab horse's life.

Skinner had a low set of cabs and a low set of drivers.

He was hard on the men, and the men were hard on the horses. In this place we had no Sunday rest, and it was in the heat of summer.

Sometimes on a Sunday morning, a party of fast men would hire the cab for the day – four of them inside and another with the driver, and I had to take them ten or fifteen miles out into the country, and back again. Never would any of them get down to walk up a hill, let it be ever so steep, or the day ever so hot – unless indeed, when the driver was afraid I should not manage it. Sometimes I was so fevered and worn that I could hardly touch my food. How I longed for the nice bran mash with nitre in it that Jerry used to give us on Saturday nights in hot weather, to cool us down and make us so comfortable! Then we had two nights and a whole day of unbroken rest, and on Monday morning we were as fresh as young horses again. But there was no rest, and my driver was just as hard as his master. He had a cruel whip with something so sharp at the end that it sometimes drew blood, and he would even whip me under the belly and flip the lash out at my head. Indignities like these took the heart out of me terribly, but still I did my best and never hung back. As poor Ginger said, it was no use; men are the strongest.

My life was now so utterly wretched that I wished I might, like Ginger, drop down dead at my work and be out of my misery. One day my wish very nearly came to pass.

I went on the stand at eight in the morning and had done a good share of work, when we had to take a fare to the railway. A long train was expected in, so my driver pulled up at the back of some of the outside cabs, to take the chance of a return fare. It was a very heavy train, and as all the cabs were soon engaged, ours was called for. There was a party of four: a noisy, blustering man with a lady, a little boy, and a young girl, and a great deal of luggage. The lady and the boy got into the cab, and while the man ordered about the luggage, the young girl came and looked at me.

'Papa,' she said. 'I am sure this poor horse cannot take us and all our luggage so far, he is so very weak and worn out. Do look at him.'

'Oh, he's all right, miss,' said my driver. 'He's strong enough.'

The porter, who was pulling about some heavy boxes, suggested to the gentleman as there was so much luggage, whether he would not take a second cab.

'Can your horse do it, or can't he?' said the man.

'Oh, he can do it all right, sir. Send up the boxes, porter. He would take more than that!' And he helped to haul up a box so heavy that I could feel the springs go down.

'Papa, Papa, do take a second cab,' said the young girl in a beseeching tone. 'I am sure we are wrong. I am sure it is very cruel.'

'Nonsense, Grace! Get in at once, and don't make all this fuss. A pretty thing it would be if a man of business had to examine every cab horse before he hired it – the man knows his business, of course. There, get in and hold your tongue!'

My gentle friend had to obey. Box after box was dragged up and lodged on the top of the cab, or settled by the side of the driver. At last all was ready, and with his usual jerk at the rein and lash of whip, he drove out of the state.

The load was very heavy, and I had had neither food nor rest since the morning; but I did my best, as I always had done, in spite of cruelty and injustice.

I got along fairly till we came to Ludgate Hill, but there the heavy load and my own exhaustion were too much. I was struggling to keep on, goaded by constant chucks of the rein and use of the whip, when in a single moment – I cannot tell how – my feet slipped from under me, and I fell heavily to the ground on my side.

The suddenness and the force with which I fell seemed to beat all the breath out of my body. I lay perfectly still. Indeed, I had no power to move, and I thought now I was going to die. I heard a sort of confusion round me, loud angry voices, and the getting down of the luggage, but it was all like a dream.

I thought I heard that sweet pitying voice saying, 'Oh! That poor horse! It is all our fault.' Someone came and loosened the throat strap of my bridle, and undid the traces which kept the collar so tight upon me. Someone said, 'He's dead. He'll never get up again.' Then I could hear the policeman giving orders, but I did not even open my eyes. I could only draw a gasping breath now and then. Some cold water was thrown over my head, and some cordial was poured into my mouth, and something was covered over me. I cannot tell how long I lay there, but I found my life coming back, and a kind-voiced man was patting me and encouraging me to rise.

After some more cordial had been given me, and after one or two attempts, I staggered to my feet, and was gently led to some stables which were close by. Here I was put into a well-littered stall, and some warm gruel was brought to me, which I drank thankfully.

In the evening I was sufficiently recovered to be led back to Skinner's stables, where I think they did the best for me they could. In the morning Skinner came with a farrier to look at me.

He examined me very closely and said, 'This is a case of overwork more than disease, and if you could give him a runoff for six months, he would be able to work again. But now there is not an ounce of strength in him.'

'Then he must just go to the dogs,' said Skinner. 'I have no meadows to nurse sick horses in – he might get well or he might not; that sort of thing don't suit my business. My plan is to work 'em as long as they'll go, and then sell 'em for what they'll fetch, at the knacker's or elsewhere.'

'If he was broken-winded,' said the farrier, 'you had better have him killed out of hand, but he is not. There is a sale of horses coming off in about ten days; if you rest him and feed him up, he may pick up, and you may get more than his skin is worth, at any rate.'

Upon this advice, Skinner, unwillingly, I think, gave orders that I should be well fed and cared for, and the stable man, happily for me, carried out the orders with a much better will than his master had in giving them. Ten days of perfect rest, plenty of good oats, hay, bran mashes with boiled linseed mixed in them, did more to get up my condition than anything else could have done. Those linseed mashes were delicious, and I began to think, after all, it might be better to live than go to the dogs. When the twelfth day after the accident came, I was taken to the sale, a few miles out of London.

I felt that any change from my present place must be an improvement, so I held up my head and hoped for the best.

At this sale, of course, I found myself in company with old broken-down horses – some lame, some broken-winded, some old, and some that I am sure it would have been merciful to shoot.

The buyers and sellers, too, many of them, looked not much better off than the poor beasts they were bargaining about. There were poor old men, trying to get a horse or a pony for a few pounds, that might drag about some little wood or coal cart. There were poor men trying to sell a worn-out beast for two or three pounds, rather than have the greater loss of killing him. Some of them looked as if poverty and hard times had hardened them all over; but there were others that I would have willingly used the last of my strength in serving – poor and shabby, but kind and human, with voices that I could trust.

There was on tottering old man that took a great

fancy to me, and I to him, but I was not strong enough –
it was an anxious time! Coming from the better part of
the fair, I noticed a man who looked like a gentleman
farmer, with a young boy by his side. He had a broad
back and round shoulders, a kind, ruddy face, and he
wore a broad-brimmed hat. When he came up to me and
my companions, he stood still and gave a pitying look
round upon us. I saw his eye rest on me. I had a good
mane and tail, which helped my appearance. I pricked
my ears and looked at him.

'There's a horse, Willie, that has known better days.'

'Poor old fellow!' said the boy. 'Do you think, Grandpapa, he was ever a carriage horse?'

'Oh, yes, my boy,' said the farmer, coming closer. 'He
might have been anything when he was young. Look at
his nostrils and his ears, the shape of his neck and
shoulder. There's a deal of breeding about that horse.'

He put out his hand and gave me a kind pat on the
neck. I put on my nose in answer to his kindness; the boy
stroked my face.

'Poor old fellow! See, Grandpapa, how well he under-
stands kindness. Could not you buy him and make him
young again, as you did with Ladybird?'

'My dear boy, I can't make all old horses young.
Besides, Ladybird was not so very old – she was run
down and badly used.'

'Well, Grandpapa, I don't believe that this one is old;
look at his mane and tail. I wish you would look into his
mouth, and then you could tell. Though he is so very
thin, his eyes are not sunk like some old horses'.'

The old gentleman laughed. 'Bless the boy! He is as
horsey as his old grandfather.'

'But do look at his mouth, Grandpapa, and ask the
price. I am sure he would grow young in our meadows.'

The man who had brought me for sale now put in his
own word.

'The young gentleman's a real knowing one, sir. Now

the fact is, this 'ere hoss is just pulled down with overwork in the cabs. He's not an old one, and I heard as how the vetenary should say that a six months' run-off would set him right up, being as how his wind was not broken. I've had the tending of him these ten days past, and a gratefuller, pleasanter animal I never met with. 'Twould be worth a gentleman's while to give a five-pound note for him and let him have a chance. I'll be bound he'd be worth twenty pounds next spring.'

The old gentleman laughed and the little boy looked up at him eagerly.

'Oh, Grandpapa, did you not say the colt sold for five pounds more than you expected? You would not be poorer if you did buy this one.'

The farmer slowly felt my legs, which were much swelled and strained; then he looked at my mouth. 'Thirteen or fourteen, I should say. Just trot him out, will you?'

I arched my poor thin neck, raised my tail a little and drew out my legs as well as I could; but they were very stiff and sore.

'What is the lowest you will take for him?' said the farmer as I came back.

'Five pounds, sir; that was the lowest price my master would set.'

''Tis a speculation,' said the old gentleman, shaking his head, but at the same time slowly drawing out his purse. 'Quite a speculation! Have you any more business here?' he said, counting the sovereigns into his hand.

'No, sir, I can take him to the inn, if you please.'

'Do so, I am now going there.'

They walked forward, and I was led behind. The boy could hardly control his delight, and the old gentleman seemed to enjoy his pleasure. I had a good feed at the inn, and was then gently ridden home by a servant of my new master's and turned into a large meadow with a shed in one corner of it.

Mr. Thoroughgood, for that was the name of my benefactor, gave orders that I should have hay and oats every night and morning, and the run of the meadow during the day. 'And you, Willie,' said he 'must take the oversight of him. I give him in charge to you.'

The boy was proud of his charge, and undertook it in all seriousness. There was not a day when he did not pay me a visit, sometimes picking me out from among the other horses, and giving me a bit of carrot or something good, or sometimes standing by me while I ate my oats. He always came with kind words and caresses, and of course I grew fond of him. He called me Old Crony, as I used to come to him in the field and follow him about. Sometimes he brought his grandfather, who always looked at my legs.

'This is our point, Willie,' he would say. 'But he is improving so steadily that I think we shall see a change for the better in the spring.'

The perfect rest, the good food, the soft turf and gentle exercise soon began to tell on my condition and my spirits. I had a good constitution from my mother, and I was never strained when I was young, so that I had a better chance than many horses who have been worked before they came to their full strength. During the winter my legs improved so much that I began to feel quite young again.

Then spring came round, and one day in March, Mr. Thoroughgood determined that he would try me in the phaeton. I was well pleased, and he and Willie drove me a few miles. My legs were not stiff now, and I did the work with perfect ease.

'He's growing young, Willie! We must give him a little gentle work now, and by mid-summer he will be as good as Ladybird. He has a beautiful mouth and good paces – they can't be better.'

'Oh, Grandpapa! How glad I am you bought him!'

'So am I, my boy, but he has to thank you more than

me. We must now be looking out for a quite genteel place for him, where he will be valued.'

One day during this summer, the groom cleaned and dressed me with such extraordinary care that I thought some new change must be at hand. He trimmed my fetlocks and legs, passed the tar-brush over my hoofs, and even parted my forelock. I think the harness had an extra polish. Willie seemed anxious, half merry, as he got into the chaise with his grandfather.

'If the ladies take to him,' said the old gentleman, 'they'll be suited, and he'll be suited. We can't but try.'

At the distance of a mile or two from the village, we came to a pretty, low house with a lawn and shrubbery at the front and a drive up to the door. Willie rang the bell and asked if Miss Blomefield or Miss Ellen was at home. Yes, they were. So, while Willie stayed with me, Mr. Thoroughgood went into the house. In about ten minutes he returned, followed by three ladies. One tall, pale lady, wrapped in a white shawl, leaned on a younger lady, with dark eyes and a merry face; the other, a very stately looking person, was Miss Blomefield. They all came and looked at me and asked questions. The younger lady – that was Miss Ellen – took to me very much; she said she was sure that she should like me, I had such a good face. The tall, pale lady said that she should always be nervous in riding behind a horse that had once been down, as I might come down again, and if I did, she should never get over the fright of it.

'You see, ladies,' said Mr. Thoroughgood, 'many first-rate horses have had their knees broken through the carelessness of their drivers, without the fault of their own, and from what I can see of this horse, I should say that is his case. But of course I do not want to influence you. If you incline, you can have him on trial, and then your coachman will see what he thinks of him.'

'You have always been such a good adviser to us about

our horses,' said the stately lady, 'that your recommendation would go a long way with me, and if my sister Lavinia sees no objection, we will accept your offer of a trial, with our thanks.'

It was then arranged that I should be sent for by them the next day.

In the morning a smart-looking young man came for me. At first, he looked pleased; but when he saw my knees, he said in a disappointed voice, 'I didn't think, sir, you would have recommended my ladies a blemished horse like that.'

'Handsome is, that handsome does,' said my master. 'You are only taking him on trial, and I am sure you will do fairly by him, young man. If he is not safe as any horse you ever drove, send him back.'

I was led home, placed in a comfortable stable, fed, and left to myself. The next day when my groom was cleaning my face, he said, 'That is just like the star that Black Beauty had. He is much the same height, too. I wonder where he is now.'

A little further on he came to the place in my neck where I was bled, and where a little knot was left in the skin. He almost started, and began to look me over carefully, talking to himself.

'White star in the forehead, one white foot on the off side, this little knot just in that place.' Then, looking at the middle of my back – 'And as I am alive, there is a little patch of white hair that John used to call "Beauty's three-penny bit." It *must* be Black Beauty! Why, Beauty! Beauty! Do you know me? Little Joe Green, that almost killed you?' And he began patting and patting me as if he was quite overjoyed.

I could not say that I remembered him, for now he was a fine grown young fellow, with black whiskers and a man's voice, but I was sure he knew me and that he was Joe Green, and I was very glad. I put my nose up to him, and tried to say that we were friends. I never saw a man so pleased.

'Give you a fair trial! I should think so indeed! I wonder who the rascal was that broke your knees, my old Beauty! You must have been badly served out somewhere. Well, it won't be my fault if you haven't good times of it now! I wish John Manly was here to see you.'

In the afternoon I was put into a low park chair and brought to the door. Miss Ellen was going to try me, and Green went with her. I soon found that she was a good driver, and she seemed pleased with my paces. I heard Joe telling her about me, and that he was sure I was Squire Gordon's old Black Beauty.

When we returned, the other sisters came out to hear how I had behaved. She told them what she had just heard, and said, 'I shall certainly write to Mrs. Gordon, and tell her that her favourite horse has come to us. How pleased she will be!'

After this I was driven every day for a week or so, and as I appeared to be quite safe, Miss Lavinia at last ventured out in the small closed carriage. After this it was quite decided to keep me and call me by my old name of Black Beauty.

I have now lived in this happy place a whole year. Joe is the best and kindest of grooms. My work is easy and pleasant, and I feel my strength and spirits all coming back again.

Mr. Thoroughgood said to Joe the other day, 'In your place he will last till he is twenty years old – perhaps more.'

Willie always speaks of me when he can and treats me as his special friend. My ladies have promised that I shall never be sold, and so I have nothing to fear. And here my story ends. My troubles are all over, and I am at home; and often before I am quite awake, I fancy I am still in the orchard at Birtwick, standing with my old friends under the apple trees.

Roy

from *All Things Bright and Beautiful*
by James Herriot

THE silver haired old gentleman with the pleasant face didn't look the type to be easily upset but his eyes glared at me angrily and his lips quivered with indignation.

'Mr Herriot,' he said. 'I have come to make a complaint. I strongly object to your allowing my dog to suffer unnecessarily.'

'Suffer? What suffering?'

'I think you know, Mr Herriot. I brought my dog in a few days ago. He was very lame and I am referring to your treatment on that occasion.'

I nodded. 'Yes, I remember it well . . . but where does the suffering come in?'

'Well, the poor animal is going around with his leg dangling and I have it on good authority that the bone is fractured and should have been put in plaster immediately.' The old gentleman stuck his chin out fiercely.

'All right, you can stop worrying,' I said. 'Your dog has a radial paralysis caused by a blow on the ribs and if you are patient and follow my treatment he'll gradually improve. In fact, I think he'll recover completely.'

'But he trails his leg when he walks.'

'I know – that's typical, and to the layman it does give the appearance of a broken leg. But he shows no sign of pain?'

'No, he seems quite happy, but this lady seemed to be absolutely sure of her facts. She was adamant.'

'Lady?'

'Yes,' said the old gentleman. 'She is very clever with animals and she came round to see if she could help in my dog's convalescence. She brought some excellent condition powders with her.'

'Ah!' A blinding shaft pierced the fog in my mind. All was suddenly clear. 'It was Mrs Donovan, wasn't it?'

'Well . . . er, yes. That was her name.'

Old Mrs Donovan was a woman who really got around. No matter what was going on in Darrowby – weddings, funerals, house-sales – you'd find the dumpy little figure and walnut face among the spectators, the darting, black-button eyes taking everything in. And always, on the end of its lead, her terrier dog.

When I say 'old', I'm guessing, because she appeared ageless; she seemed to have been around a long time but she could have been anything between fifty five and seventy five. She certainly had the vitality of a young woman because she must have walked vast distances in her dedicated quest to keep abreast of events. Many people took an uncharitable view of her acute curiosity but whatever the motivation, her activities took her into almost every channel of life in the town. One of these channels was our veterinary practice.

Because Mrs Donovan, among her other widely ranging interests, was an animal doctor. In fact I think it would be safe to say that this facet of her life transcended all the others.

She could talk at length on the ailments of small animals and she had a whole armoury of medicines and remedies at her command, her two specialities being her miracle working condition powders and a dog shampoo of unprecedented value for improving the coat. She had an uncanny ability to sniff out a sick animal and it was not uncommon when I was on my rounds to find Mrs Donovan's dark gipsy face posed intently over what I had thought was my patient while she administered calf's foot jelly or one of her own patent nostrums.

I suffered more than Siegfried because I took a more active part in the small animal side of our practice. I was anxious to develop this aspect and to improve my image in this field and Mrs Donovan didn't help at all. 'Young Mr Herriot,' she would confide to my clients, 'is all right with cattle and such like, but he don't know nothing about dogs and cats.'

And of course they believed her and had implicit faith in her. She had the irresistible mystic appeal of the amateur and on top of that there was her habit, particularly endearing in Darrowby, of never charging for her advice, her medicines, her long periods of diligent nursing.

Older folk in the town told how her husband, an Irish farm worker, had died many years ago and how he must have had a 'bit put away' because Mrs Donovan had apparently been able to indulge all her interests over the years without financial strain. Since she inhabited the streets of Darrowby all day and every day I often encountered her and she always smiled up at me sweetly and told me how she had been sitting up all night with Mrs So-and-so's dog that I'd been treating. She felt sure she'd be able to pull it through.

There was no smile on her face, however, on the day when she rushed into the surgery while Siegfried and I were having tea.

'Mr Herriot!' she gasped. 'Can you come? My little dog's been run over!'

I jumped up and ran out to the car with her. She sat in

the passenger seat with her head bowed, her hands clasped tightly on her knees.

'He slipped his collar and ran in front of a car,' she murmured.

'He's lying in front of the school half way up Cliffend Road. Please hurry.'

I was there within three minutes but as I bent over the dusty little body stretched on the pavement I knew there was nothing I could do. The fast-glazing eyes, the faint, gasping respirations, the ghastly pallor of the mucous membranes all told the same story.

I'll take him back to the surgery and get some saline into him, Mrs Donovan,' I said. 'But I'm afraid he's had a massive internal haemorrhage. Did you see what happened exactly?'

She gulped. 'Yes, the wheel went right over him.'

Ruptured liver, for sure. I passed my hands under the little animal and began to lift him gently, but as I did so the breathing stopped and the eyes stared fixedly ahead.

Mrs Donovan sank to her knees and for a few moments she gently stroked the rough hair of the head and chest. 'He's dead, isn't he?' she whispered at last.

'I'm afraid he is,' I said.

She got slowly to her feet and stood bewilderedly among the little group of bystanders on the pavement. Her lips moved but she seemed unable to say any more.

I took her arm, led her over to the car and opened the door. 'Get in and sit down,' I said. 'I'll run you home. Leave everything to me.'

I wrapped the dog in my calving overall and laid him in the boot before driving away. It wasn't until we drew up outside Mrs Donovan's house that she began to weep silently. I sat there without speaking till she had finished. Then she wiped her eyes and turned to me.

'Do you think he suffered at all?'

'I'm certain he didn't. It was all so quick – he wouldn't know a thing about it.'

She tried to smile. 'Poor little Rex, I don't know what I'm going to do without him. We've travelled a few miles together, you know.'

'Yes, you have. He had a wonderful life, Mrs Donovan. And let me give you a bit of advice – you must get another dog. You'd be lost without one.'

She shook her head. 'No. I couldn't. That little dog meant too much to me. I couldn't let another take his place.'

'Well I know that's how you feel just now but I wish you'd think about it. I don't want to seem callous – I tell everybody this when they lose an animal and I know it's good advice.'

'Mr Herriot, I'll never have another one.' She shook her head again, very decisively. 'Rex was my faithful friend for many years and I just want to remember him. He's the last dog I'll ever have.'

I often saw Mrs Donovan around the town after this and I was glad to see she was still as active as ever, though she looked strangely incomplete without the little dog on its lead. But it must have been over a month before I had the chance to speak to her.

It was on the afternoon that Inspector Halliday of the R.S.P.C.A. rang me.

'Mr Herriot,' he said, 'I'd like you to come and see an animal with me. A cruelty case.'

'Right, what is it?'

'A dog, and it's pretty grim. A dreadful case of neglect.' He gave me the name of a row of old brick cottages down by the river and said he'd meet me there.

Halliday was waiting for me, smart and business-like in his dark uniform, as I pulled up in the back lane behind the houses. He was a big, blond man with cheerful eyes but he didn't smile as he came over to the car.

'He's in here,' he said, and led the way towards one of

the doors in the long, crumbling wall. A few curious people were hanging around and with a feeling of inevitability I recognised a gnome-like brown face. Trust Mrs Donovan, I thought, to be among those present at a time like this.

We went through the door into the long garden. I had found that even the lowliest dwellings in Darrowby had long strips of land at the back as though the builders had taken it for granted that the country people who were going to live in them would want to occupy themselves with the pursuits of the soil; with vegetable and fruit growing, even stock keeping in a small way. You usually found a pig there, a few hens, often pretty beds of flowers.

But this garden was a wilderness. A chilling air of desolation hung over the few gnarled apple and plum trees standing among a tangle of rank grass as though the place had been forsaken by all living creatures.

Halliday went over to a ramshackle wooden shed with peeling paint and a rusted corrugated iron roof. He produced a key, unlocked the padlock and dragged the door partly open. There was no window and it wasn't easy to identify the jumble inside; broken gardening tools, an ancient mangle, rows of flower pots and partly used paint tins. And right at the back, a dog sitting quietly.

I didn't notice him immediately because of the gloom and because the smell in the shed started me coughing, but as I drew closer I saw that he was a big animal, sitting very upright, his collar secured by a chain to a ring in the wall. I had seen some thin dogs but this advanced emaciation reminded me of my text books on anatomy; nowhere else did the bones of pelvis, face and rib cage stand out with such horrifying clarity. A deep, smoothed out hollow in the earth floor showed where he had lain, moved about, in fact lived for a very long time.

The sight of the animal had a stupefying effect on me;

I only half took in the rest of the scene – the filthy shreds of sacking scattered nearby, the bowl of scummy water.

'Look at his back end,' Halliday muttered.

I carefully raised the dog from his sitting position and realised that the stench in the place was not entirely due to the piles of excrement. The hind-quarters were a welter of pressure sores which had turned gangrenous and strips of sloughing tissue hung down from them. There were similar sores along the sternum and ribs.

The coat, which seemed to be a dull yellow, was matted and caked with dirt.

The Inspecter spoke again. 'I don't think he's ever been out of here. He's only a young dog – about a year old – but I understand he's been in this shed since he was an eight week old pup. Somebody out in the lane heard a whimper or he'd never have been found.'

I felt a tightening of the throat and a sudden nausea which wasn't due to the smell. It was the thought of this patient animal sitting starved and forgotten in the darkness and filth for a year. I looked again at the dog and saw in his eyes only a calm trust. Some dogs would have barked their heads off and soon been discovered, some would have become terrified and vicious, but this was one of the totally. undemanding kind, the kind which had complete faith in people and accepted all their actions without complaint. Just an occasional whimper perhaps as he sat interminably in the empty blackness which had been his world and at times wondered what it was all about.

'Well, Inspector, I hope you're going to throw the book at whoever's responsible,' I said.

Halliday grunted. 'Oh, there won't be much done. It's a case of diminished responsiblity. The owner's definitely simple. Lives with an aged mother who hardly knows what's going on either. I've seen the fellow and it seems he threw in a bit of food when he felt like it and that's about all he did. They'll fine him and stop him keeping an animal in the future but nothing more than that.'

'I see.' I reached out and stroked the dog's head and he immediately responded by resting a paw on my wrist. There was a pathetic dignity about the way he held himself erect, the calm eyes regarding me, friendly and unafraid. 'Well, you'll let me know if you want me in court.'

'Of course, and thank you for coming along.' Halliday

hesitated for a moment. 'And now I expect you'll want to put this poor thing out of his misery right away.'

I continued to run my hand over the head and ears while I thought for a moment. 'Yes . . . yes, I suppose so. We'd never find a home for him in this state. It's the kindest thing to do. Anyway, push the door wide open will you so that I can get a proper look at him.'

In the improved light I examined him more thoroughly. Perfect teeth, well-proportioned limbs with a fringe of yellow hair. I put my stethoscope on his chest and as I listened to the slow, strong thudding of the heart the dog again put his paw on my hand.

I turned to Halliday. 'You know, Inspector, inside this bag of bones there's a lovely healthy Golden Retriever. I wish there was some way of letting him out.'

As I spoke I noticed there was more than one figure in the door opening. A pair of black pebble eyes were peering intently at the dog from behind the Inspector's broad back. The other spectators had remained in the lane but Mrs Donovan's curiosity had been too much for her. I continued conversationally as though I hadn't seen her.

'You know, what this dog needs first of all is a good shampoo to clean up his matted coat.'

'Huh?' said Halliday.

'Yes. And then he wants a long course of some really strong condition powders.'

'What's that?' The Inspector looked startled.

'There's no doubt about it,' I said. 'It's the only hope for him, but where are you going to find such things? Really powerful enough, I mean.' I sighed and straightened up. 'Ah well, I suppose there's nothing else for it. I'd better put him to sleep right away. I'll get the things from my car.'

When I got back to the shed Mrs Donovan was already inside examining the dog despite the feeble remonstrances of the big man.

'Look!' she said excitedly, pointing to a name roughly scratched on the collar. 'His name's Roy.' She smiled up at me. 'It's a bit like Rex, isn't it, that name.'

'You know, Mrs Donovan, now you mention it, it is. It's very like Rex, the way it comes off your tongue.' I nodded seriously.

She stood silent for a few moments, obviously in the grip of a deep emotion, then she burst out.

'Can I have 'im? I can make him better, I know I can. Please, please let me have 'im!'

'Well I don't know,' I said. 'It's really up to the Inspector. You'll have to get his permission.'

Halliday looked at her in bewilderment, then he said: 'Excuse me, Madam,' and drew me to one side. We walked a few yards through the long grass and stopped under a tree.

'Mr Herriot,' he whispered, 'I don't know what's going on here, but I can't just pass over an animal in this condition to anybody who has a casual whim. The poor beggar's had one bad break already – I think it's enough. This woman doesn't look a suitable person . . .'

I held up a hand. 'Believe me, Inspector, you've nothing to worry about. She's a funny old stick but she's been sent from heaven today. If anybody in Darrowby can give this dog a new life it's her.'

Halliday still looked very doubtful. 'But I still don't get it. What was all that stuff about him needing shampoos and condition powders?'

'Oh never mind about that. I'll tell you some other time. What he needs is lots of good grub, care and affection and that's just what he'll get. You can take my word for it.'

'All right, you seem very sure.' Halliday looked at me for a second or two then turned and walked over to the eager little figure by the shed.

I had never before been deliberately on the look out for

Mrs Donovan: she had just cropped up wherever I happened to be, but now I scanned the streets of Darrowby anxiously day by day without sighting her. I didn't like it when Gobber Newhouse got drunk and drove his bicycle determinedly through a barrier into a ten foot hole where they were laying the new sewer and Mrs Donovan was not in evidence among the happy crowd who watched the council workmen and two policemen trying to get him out; and when she was nowhere to be seen when they had to fetch the fire engine to the fish and chip shop the night the fat burst into flames, I became seriously worried.

Maybe I should have called round to see how she was getting on with that dog. Certainly I had trimmed off the necrotic tissue and dressed the sores before she took him away, but perhaps he needed something more than that. And yet at the time I had felt a strong conviction that the main thing was to get him out of there and clean him and feed him and nature would do the rest. And I had a lot of faith in Mrs Donovan – far more than she had in me – when it came to animal doctoring; it was hard to believe I'd been completely wrong.

It must have been nearly three weeks and I was on the point of calling at her home when I noticed her stumping briskly along the far side of the market place, peering closely into every shop window exactly as before. The only difference was that she had a big yellow dog on the end of the lead.

I turned the wheel and sent my car bumping over the cobbles till I was abreast of her. When she saw me getting out she stopped and smiled impishly but she didn't speak as I bent over Roy and examined him. He was still a skinny dog but he looked bright and happy, his wounds were healthy and granulating and there was not a speck of dirt in his coat or on his skin. I knew then what Mrs Donovan had been doing all this time; she had been washing and combing and teasing at that filthy tangle till she had finally conquered it.

As I straightened up she seized my wrist in a grip of surprising strength and looked up into my eyes.

'Now Mr Herriot,' she said. 'Haven't I made a difference to this dog!'

'You've done wonders, Mrs Donovan.' I said. 'And you've been at him with that marvellous shampoo of yours, haven't you?'

She giggled and walked away and from that day I saw the two of them frequently but at a distance and something like two months went by before I had a chance to talk to her again. She was passing by the surgery as I was coming down the steps and again she grabbed my wrist.

'Mr Herriot,' she said, just as she had done before. 'Haven't I made a difference to this dog!'

I looked down at Roy with something akin to awe. He had grown and filled out and his coat, no longer yellow but a rich gold, lay in luxuriant shining swathes over the well-fleshed ribs and back. A new, brightly studded collar glittered on his neck and his tail, beautifully fringed, fanned the air gently. He was now a Golden Retriever in full magnificence. As I stared at him he reared up, plunked his fore paws on my chest and looked into my face, and in his eyes I read plainly the same calm affection and trust I had seen back in that black, noisome shed.

'Mrs Donovan,' I said softly, 'he's the most beautiful dog in Yorkshire.' Then, because I knew she was waiting for it. 'It's those wonderful condition powders. Whatever do you put in them?'

'Ah, wouldn't you like to know!' She bridled and smiled up at me coquettishly and indeed she was nearer being kissed at that moment than for many years.

I suppose you could say that that was the start of Roy's second life. And as the years passed I often pondered on the beneficent providence which had decreed that an animal which had spent his first twelve months abandoned and unwanted, staring uncomprehendingly into that unchanging, stinking darkness, should be whisked in a moment into an existence of light and movement and love. Because I don't think any dog had it quite so good as Roy from then on.

His diet changed dramatically from odd bread crusts to best stewing steak and biscuit, meaty bones and a bowl of warm milk every evening. And he never missed a thing. Garden fetes, school sports, evictions, gymkhanas – he'd be there. I was pleased to note that as time went on Mrs Donovan seemed to be clocking up an even greater daily mileage. Her expenditure on shoe leather must have been phenomenal, but of course it was absolute pie for Roy – a busy round in the morning, home for a meal then straight out again; it was all go.

Mrs Donovan didn't confine her activities to the town centre; there was a big stretch of common land down by the river where there were seats, and people used to take their dogs for a gallop and she liked to get down there fairly regularly to check on the latest developments on the domestic scene. I often saw Roy loping majestically over the grass among a pack of assorted canines, and when he wasn't doing that he was submitting to being stroked or patted or generally fussed over. He was handsome and he just liked people; it made him irresistible.

It was common knowledge that his mistress had bought a whole selection of brushes and combs of various sizes with which she laboured over his coat. Some people said she had a little brush for his teeth, too, and it might have been true, but he certainly wouldn't need his nails clipped – his life on the roads would keep them down.

Mrs Donovan, too, had her reward; she had a faithful companion by her side every hour of the day and night. But there was more to it than that; she had always had the compulsion to help and heal animals and the salvation of Roy was the high point of her life – a blazing triumph which never dimmed.

I know the memory of it was always fresh because many years later I was sitting on the sidelines at a cricket match and I saw the two of them; the old lady glancing keenly around her, Roy glazing placidly out at the field of play, apparently enjoying every ball. At the end of the match I watched them move away with the dispersing crowd; Roy would be about twelve then and heaven only knows how old Mrs Donovan must have been, but the big golden animal was trotting along effortlessly and his mistress, a little more bent, perhaps, and her head rather nearer the ground, was going very well.

When she saw me she came over and I felt the familiar tight grip on my wrist.

'Mr Herriot,' she said, and in the dark probing eyes the pride was still as warm, the triumph still as bursting new as if it had all happened yesterday.

'Mr Herriot, haven't I made a difference to this dog!'

How the Leopard got his Spots

from *Just So Stories*
by Rudyard Kipling

IN the days when everybody started fair, Best Beloved, the Leopard lived in a place called the High Veldt. 'Member it wasn't the Low Veldt, or the Bush Veldt, or the Sour Veldt, but the 'sclusively bare, hot, shiny High Veldt, where there was sand and sandy-coloured rock and 'sclusively tufts of sandy-yellowish grass. The Giraffe and the Zebra and the Eland and the Koodoo and the Hartebeest lived there; and they were 'sclusively sandy-yellow-brownish all over; but the Leopard, he was the 'sclusivest sandiest-yellowish-brownest of them all — a greyish-yellowish catty-shaped kind of beast, and he matched the 'sclusively yellowish-greyish-brownish colour of the High Veldt to one hair. This was very bad for the Giraffe and the Zebra and the rest of them; for he would lie down by a 'sclusively yellowish-greyish-brownish stone or clump of grass, and when the Giraffe or the Zebra or the Eland or the Koodoo or the Bush-Buck or the Bonte-Buck came by he would surprise them out of their jumpsome lives. He would indeed! And, also, there was an Ethiopian with bows and arrows (a 'sclusively greyish-brownish-yellowish man he was then), who lived on the High Veldt with the Leopard; and the two used to hunt together – the Ethiopian with his bows and arrows, and the Leopard 'sclusively with his teeth and claws – till the Giraffe and the Eland and the Koodoo and the Quagga and all the rest of them didn't know which way to jump, Best Beloved. They didn't indeed!

After a long time – things lived for ever so long in those days – they learned to avoid anything that looked like a Leopard or an Ethiopian; and bit by bit – the Giraffe began it, because his legs were the longest – they went away from the High Veldt. They scuttled for days and days and days till they came to a great forest, 'sclusively full of trees and bushes and stripy, speckly, patchy-blatchy shadows, and there they hid: and after another long time, what with standing half in the shade and half out of it, and what with the slippery-slidy shadows of the trees falling on them, the Giraffe grew blotchy, and the Zebra grew stripy, and the Eland and the Koodoo grew darker, with little wavy grey lines on their backs like bark on a tree-trunk; and so, though you could hear them and smell them, you could very seldom see them, and then only when you knew precisely where to look. They had a beautiful time in the 'sclusively speckly-spickly shadows of the forest, while the Leopard and the Ethiopian ran about over the 'sclusively greyish-yellowish-reddish High Veldt outside, wondering where all their breakfasts and their dinners and their teas had gone. At last they were so hungry that they ate rats and beetles and rock-rabbits, the Leopard and the Ethiopian, and then they met Baviaan – the dog-headed, barking Baboon, who is Quite the Wisest Animal in All South Africa.

Said Leopard to Baviaan (and it was a very hot day), 'Where has all the game gone?'

And Baviaan winked. *He* knew.

Said the Ethiopian to Baviaan, 'Can you tell me the present habitat of the aboriginal Fauna?' (That meant just the same thing, but the Ethiopian always used long words. He was a grown-up.)

And Baviaan winked. *He* knew.

Then said Baviaan, 'The game has gone into other spots; and my advice to you, Leopard, is to go into other spots as soon as you can.'

And the Ethiopian said, 'That is all very fine, but I wish to know whither the aboriginal Fauna has migrated.'

Then said Baviaan, 'The aborignal Fauna has joined the aboriginal Flora because it was high time for a change; and my advice to you, Ethiopian, is to change as soon as you can.'

That puzzled the Leopard and the Ethiopian, but they set off to look for the aboriginal Flora, and presently, after ever so many days, they saw a great, high, tall forest full of tree-trunks all 'sclusively speckled and sprottled and spottled, dotted and splashed and slashed and hatched and cross-hatched with shadows. (Say that quickly aloud, and you will see how *very* shadowy the forest must have been.)

'What is this,' said the Leopard, 'that is so 'sclusively dark, and yet so full of little pieces of light?'

'I don't know,' said the Ethiopian, 'but it ought to be the aboriginal Flore. I can smell Giraffe, and I can hear Giraffe, but I can't see Giraffe.'

'That's curious,' said the Leopard. 'I suppose it is because we have just come in out of the sunshine. I can smell Zebra, and I can hear Zebra, but I can't see Zebra.'

'Wait a bit,' said the Ethiopian. 'It's a long time since we've hunted 'em. Perhaps we've forgotten what they were like.'

'Fiddle!' said the Leopard. 'I remember them perfectly on the High Veldt, especially their marrow-bones. Giraffe is about seventeen feet high, of a 'sclusively fulvous golden-yellow from head to heel; and Zebra is about four and a half feet high, of a 'sclusively grey-fawn colour from head to heel.'

'Umm,' said the Ethiopian, looking into the speckly-spickly shadows of the aboriginal Flora-forest. 'Then they ought to show up in this dark place like ripe bananas in a smoke-house.'

But they didn't. The Leopard and the Ethiopian hunted all day; and though they could smell them and hear them, they never saw one of them.

'For goodness' sake,' said the Leopard at tea-time, 'let us wait till it gets dark. This daylight hunting is a perfect scandal.'

So they waited till dark, and then the Leopard heard something breathing sniffily in the starlight that fell all stripy through the branches, and he jumped at the noise, and it smelt like Zebra, and it felt like Zebra, and when he knocked it down it kicked like Zebra, but he couldn't see it. So he said, 'Be quiet, O you person without any form. I am going to sit on your head till morning, because there is something about you that I don't understand.'

Presently he heard a grunt and a crash and a scramble, and the Ethiopian called out, 'I've caught a thing and I can't see. It smells like Giraffe, and it kicks like Giraffe, but it hasn't any form.'

'Don't you trust it,' said the Leopard. 'Sit on its head till the morning – same as me. They haven't any form – any of 'em.'

So they sat down on them hard till bright morning-time, and then Leopard said, 'What have you at your end of the table, Brother?'

The Ethiopian scratched his head and said, 'It ought to be 'sclusively a rich fulvous orange-tawny from head to heel, and it ought to be Giraffe; but it is covered all over with chestnut blotches. What have you at *your* end of the table, Brother?'

And the Leopard scratched his head and said, 'It ought to be 'sclusively a delicate greyish-fawn, and it ought to be Zebra; but it is covered all over with black and purple stripes. What in the world have you been doing to yourself, Zebra? Don't you know that if you were on the High Veldt I could see you ten miles off? You haven't any form.'

'Yes,' said the Zebra, 'but this isn't the High Veldt. Can't you see?'

'I can now,' said the Leopard. 'But I couldn't all yesterday. How is it done?'

'Let us up,' said the Zebra, 'and we will show you.'

They let the Zebra and the Giraffe get up; and Zebra moved away to some little thorn-bushes where the sunlight fell all stripy, and Giraffe moved off to some tallish trees where the shadows fell all blotchy.

'Now watch,' said the Zebra and the Giraffe. 'This is the way it's done. One – two – three! And where's your breakfast?'

Leopard stared, and Ethiopian stared, but all they could see were stripy shadows and blotched shadows in the forest, but never a sign of Zebra and Giraffe. They had just walked off and hidden themselves in the shadowy forest.

'Hi! Hi!' said the Ethiopian. 'That's a trick worth learning. Take a lesson by it, Leopard. You show up in this dark place like a bar of soap in a coal-scuttle.'

'Ho! Ho!' said the Leopard. 'Would it surprise you very much to know that you show up in this dark place like a mustard-plaster on a sack of coals?'

'Well, calling names won't catch dinner,' said the Ethiopian. 'The long and the little of it is that we don't match our backgrounds. I'm going to take Baviaan's advice. He told me I ought to change; and as I've nothing to change except my skin I'm going to change that.'

'What to?' said the Leopard, tremendously excited.

This is Wise Baviaan, the dog-headed Baboon, who is Quite the Wisest Animal in All South Africa. I have drawn him from a statue that I made up out of my own head, and I have written his name on his belt and on his shoulder and on the thing he is sitting on. I have written it in what is not called Coptic and Hieroglyphic and Cuneiformic and Bengalic and Burmic and Hebric, all because he is so wise. He is not beautiful, but he is very wise; and I should like to paint him with paint-box colours, but I am not allowed. The umbrella-ish thing about his head is his Conventional Mane.

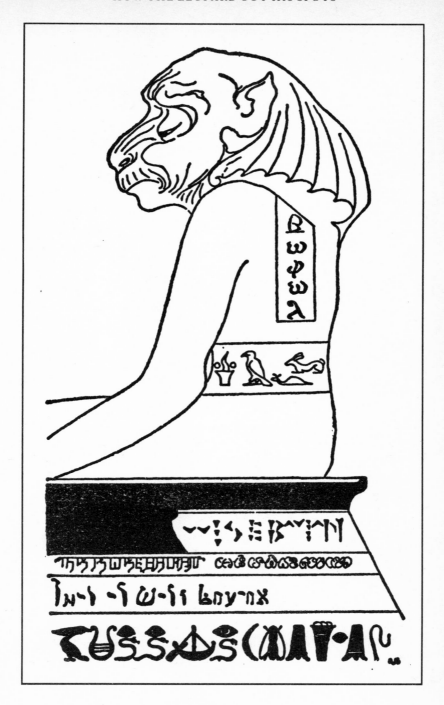

'To a nice working blackish-brownish colour, with a little purple in it, and touches of slaty-blue. It will be the very thing for hiding in hollows and behind trees.'

So he changed his skin then and there, and the Leopard was more excited than ever; he had never seen a man change his skin before.

'But what about me?' he said, when the Ethiopian had worked his last little finger into his fine new black skin.

'You take Baviaan's advice too. He told you to go into spots.'

'So I did,' said the Leopard. 'I went into other spots as fast as I could. I went into this spot with you, and a lot of good it has done me.'

'Oh,' said the Ethiopian, 'Baviaan didn't mean spots in South Africa. He meant spots on your skin.'

'What's the use of that?' said the Leopard.

'Think of Giraffe,' said the Ethiopian. 'Or if you prefer stripes, think of Zebra. They find their spots and stripes give them per-fect satisfaction.'

'Umm,' said the Leopard. 'I wouldn't look like Zebra – not for ever so.'

'Well, make up your mind,' said the Ethiopian, 'because I'd hate to go hunting without you, but I must if you insist on looking like a sunflower against a tarred fence.'

'I'll take spots, then,' said the Leopard; 'but don't make 'em too vulgar-big. I wouldn't look like Giraffe – not for ever so.'

'I'll make 'em with the tips of my fingers,' said the Ethiopian. 'There's plenty of black left on my skin still. Stand over!'

Then the Ethiopian put his five fingers close together (there was plenty of black left on his new skin still) and pressed them all over the leopard, and wherever the five fingers touched they left five little black marks, all close together. You can see them on any Leopard's skin you like, Best Beloved. Sometimes the fingers slipped and the marks got a little blurred; but if you look closely at any Leopard now you will see that there are always five spots – off five fat black finger-tips.

'Now you *are* a beauty!' said the Ethiopian. 'You can lie out on the bare ground and look like a heap of pebbles. You can lie out on the naked rocks and look like a piece of pudding-stone. You can lie out on a leafy branch and look like sunshine sifting through the leaves; and you can lie right across the centre of a path and look like nothing in particular. Think of that and purr!'

'But if I'm all this,' said the Leopard, 'why didn't you go spotty too?'

'Oh, plain black's best for a nigger,' said the Ethiopian. 'Now come along and we'll see if we can't get even with Mr One-Two-Three-Where's-your-Breakfast!'

So they went away and lived happily ever afterward, Best Beloved. That is all.

Oh, now and then you will hear grown-ups say, 'Can the Ethiopian change his skin or the Leopard his spots?' I don't think even grown-ups would keep on saying such a silly thing if the Leopard and the Ethiopian hadn't done it once – do you? But they will never do it again, Best Beloved. They are quite contented as they are.

The Cat that Walked by Himself

from *Animal Stories*
by Rudyard Kipling

HEAR and attend and listen; for this befell and behappened and became and was, O my Best Beloved, when the Tame animals were wild. The Dog was wild, and the Horse was wild, and the Cow was wild, and the Sheep was wild, and the Pig was wild – as wild as wild could be – and they walked in the Wet Wild Woods by their wild lones. But the wildest of all the wild animals was the Cat. He walked by himself, and all places were alike to him.

Of course the Man was wild too. He was dreadfully wild. He didn't even begin to be tame till he met the Woman, and she told him that she did not like living in his wild ways. She picked out a nice dry Cave, instead of a heap of wet leaves, to lie down in; and she strewed clean sand on the floor; and she lit a nice fire of wood at the back of the Cave; and she hung a dried wild-horse skin, tail-down, across the opening of the Cave; and she said 'Wipe your feet, dear, when you come in, and now we'll keep house.'

That night, Best Beloved, they ate wild sheep roasted

on the hot stones, and flavoured with wild garlic and wild pepper; and wild duck stuffed with wild rice and wild fenugreek and wild coriander; and marrow-bones of wild oxen; and wild cherries and wild grenadillas. Then the Man went to sleep in front of the fire ever so happy; but the Woman sat up, combing her hair. She took the bone of the shoulder of mutton – the big flat blade-bone – and she looked at the wonderful marks on it, and she threw more wood on the fire, and she made a Magic. She made the First Singing Magic in the world.

Out in the Wet Wild Wood all the wild animals gathered together where they could see the light of the fire a long way off, and they wondered what it meant.

Then Wild Horse stamped with his wild foot and said, 'O my Friends and O my Enemies, why have the Man and Woman made that great light in that great Cave, and what harm will it do us?'

Wild Dog lifted up his wild nose and smelled the smell of the roast mutton, and said, 'I will go up and see and look, and say; for I think it is good. Cat, come with me.'

'Nenni!' said the Cat. 'I am the Cat who walks by himself, and all places are alike to me, I will not come.'

'Then we can never be friends again,' said Wild Dog, and he trotted off to the Cave. But when he had gone a little way the Cat said to himself, 'All places are alike to me. Why should I not go too and see and look and come away at my own liking?' So he slipped after Wild Dog softly, very softly, and hid himself where he could hear everything.

When Wild Dog reached the mouth of the Cave he lifted up the dried horse-skin with his nose and sniffed the beautiful smell of the roast mutton, and the Woman, looking at the blade-bone, heard him, and laughed, and said, 'Here comes the first, Wild Thing out of the Wild Woods, what do you want?'

Wild Dog said, 'O my Enemy and Wife of my Enemy, what is this that smells so good in the Wild Woods?'

Then the Woman picked up a roasted mutton-bone and threw it to Wild Dog, and said, 'Wild Thing out of the Wild Woods, taste and try.' Wild Dog gnawed the bone, and it was more delicious than anything he had ever tasted, and he said, 'O my Enemy and Wife of my Enemy, give me another.'

The Woman said 'Wild Thing out of the Wild Woods, help my Man to hunt through the day and guard this Cave at night, and I will give you as many roast bones as you need.'

'Ah!' said the Cat, listening. 'This is a very foolish Dog.' And he went back through the Wet Wild Woods waving his wild tail, and walking by his wild lone. But he never told anybody.

When the Man woke up he said, 'What is Wild Dog doing here?' And the Woman said, 'His name is not Wild Dog any more, but the First Friend, because he will be our friend for always and always and always. Take him with you when you go hunting.'

Next night the Woman cut great green armfuls of fresh grass from the water-meadows, and dried it before the fire, so that it smelt like new-mown hay, and she sat at the mouth of the Cave and plaited a halter out of horse-hide, and she looked at the shoulder-of-mutton bone – at the big broad blade-bone – and she made a Magic. She made the Second Singing Magic in the world.

Out in the Wild Woods all the wild animals wondered what had happened to Wild Dog, and at last Wild Horse stamped with his foot and said, 'I will go and see and say why Wild Dog has not returned. Cat, come with me.'

'Nenni!' said the Cat. 'I am the Cat who walks by himself, and all places are alike to me. I will not come.' But all the same he followed Wild Horse softly, very softly, and hid himself where he could hear everything.

When the Woman heard Wild Horse tripping and stumbling on his long mane, she laughed and said, 'Here

comes the second, Wild Thing out of the Wild Woods, what do you want?'

Wild Horse said, 'O my Enemy and Wife of my Enemy, where is Wild Dog?'

The Woman laughed, and picked up the blade-bone and looked at it, and said, 'Wild Thing out of the Wild Woods, you did not come here for Wild Dog, but for the sake of this good grass.'

And Wild Horse, tripping and stumbling on his long mane, said, 'That is true; give it me to eat.'

The Woman said, 'Wild Thing out of the Wild Woods, bend your wild head and wear what I give you, and you shall eat the wonderful grass three times a day.'

'Ah!' said the Cat, listening. 'This is a clever Woman, but she is not so clever as I am.'

Wild Horse bent his wild head, and the Woman slipped the plaited-hide halter over it, and Wild Horse breathed on the Woman's feet and said, 'O my Mistress, and Wife of my Master, I will be your servant for the sake of the wonderful grass.'

'Ah!' said the Cat, listening. 'That is a very foolish Horse.' And he went back through the Wet Wild Woods, waving his wild tail and walking by his wild lone. But he never told anybody.

When the Man and the Dog came back from hunting, the Man said, 'What is Wild Horse doing here?' And the Woman said, 'His name is not Wild Horse any more, but the First Servant, because he will carry us from place to place for always and always and always. Ride on his back when you go hunting.'

Next day, holding her wild head high that her wild horns should not catch in the wild trees, Wild Cow came up to the Cave, and the Cat followed, and hid himself just the same as before; and everything happened just the same as before; and the Cat said the same things as before; and when Wild Cow had promised to give her milk to the Woman every day in exchange for the wonderful grass, the Cat went back through the Wet Wild Woods waving his wild tail and walking by his wild lone, just the same as before. But he never told anybody. And when the Man and the Horse and the Dog came home from hunting and asked the same questions same as before, the Woman said, 'Her name is not Wild Cow any more, but the Giver of Good Food. She will give us the warm white milk for always and always and always, and I will take care of her while you and the First Friend and the First Servant go hunting.'

Next day the Cat waited to see if any other Wild Thing would go up to the Cave, but no one moved in the Wet Wild Woods, so the Cat walked there by himself; and he saw the Woman milking the Cow, and he saw the light of the fire in the Cave, and he smelt the smell of the warm white milk.

Cat said, 'O my Enemy and Wife of my Enemy, where did Wild Cow go?'

The Woman laughed and said, 'Wild Thing out of the Wild Woods, go back to the Woods again, for I have braided up my hair, and I have put away the magic blade-bone, and we have no more need of either friends or servants in our Cave.'

Cat said, 'I am not a friend, and I am not a servant, I am the Cat who walks by himself, and I wish to come into your Cave.'

Woman said, 'Then why did you not come with First Friend on the first night?'

Cat grew very angry and said, 'Has Wild Dog told tales of me?'

Then the Woman laughed and said, 'You are the Cat who walks by himself, and all places are alike to you. You are neither a friend nor a servant. You have said it yourself. Go away and walk by yourself in all places alike.'

Then Cat pretended to be sorry and said, 'Must I never come into the Cave? Must I never sit by the warm fire? Must I never drink the warm white milk? You are very wise and very beautiful. You should not be cruel even to a Cat.'

Woman said, 'I knew I was wise, but I did not know I was beautiful. So I will make a bargain with you. If ever I say one word in your praise, you may come into the Cave.'

'And if you say two words in my praise?' said the Cat.

'I never shall,' said the Woman, 'but if I say three words in your praise, you may drink the warm white milk three times a day for always and always and always.'

Then the Cat arched his back and said, 'Now let the Curtain at the mouth of the Cave, and the Fire at the back of the Cave, and the Milk-pots that stand beside the Fire, remember what my Enemy and the Wife of my Enemy has said.' And he went away through the Wet Wild Woods waving his wild tail and walking by his wild lone.

That night when the Man and the Horse and the Dog came home from hunting, the Woman did not tell them of the bargain that she had made with the Cat, because she was afraid that they might not like it.

Cat went far and far away and hid himself in the Wet Wild Woods by his wild lone for a long time till the Woman forgot all about him. Only the Bat – the little upside-down Bat – that hung inside the Cave knew where Cat hid; and every evening Bat would fly to Cat with news of what was happening.

One evening Bat said, 'There is a Baby in the Cave. He is new and pink and fat and small, and the Woman is very fond of him.'

'Ah,' said the Cat, listening. 'But what is the Baby fond of?'

'He is fond of things that are soft and tickle,' said the Bat. 'He is fond of warm things to hold in his arms when he goes to sleep. He is fond of being played with. He is fond of all those things.'

'Ah,' said the Cat, listening. 'Then my time has come.'

Next night Cat walked through the Wet Wild Woods and hid very near the Cave till morning-time, and Man and Dog and Horse went hunting. The Woman was busy cooking that morning, and the Baby cried and interrupted. So she carried him outside the Cave and gave him a handful of pebbles to play with. But still the Baby cried.

Then the Cat put out his paddy paw and patted the Baby on the cheek, and it cooed; and the Cat rubbed against its fat knees and tickled it under its fat chin with his tail. And the Baby laughed; and the Woman heard him and smiled.

Then the Bat – the little upside-down Bat – that hung in the mouth of the Cave said, 'O my Hostess and Wife of my Host and Mother of my Host's Son, a Wild Thing from the Wild Woods is most beautifully playing with your Baby.'

'A blessing on that Wild Thing whoever he may be,' said the Woman, straightening her back, 'for I was a busy woman this morning and he has done me a service.'

That very minute and second, Best Beloved, the dried horse-skin Curtain that was stretched tail-down at the mouth of the Cave fell down – *woosh!* – because it remembered the bargain she had made with the Cat; and when the Woman went to pick it up – lo and behold! – the Cat was sitting quite comfy inside the Cave.

'O my Enemy and Wife of my Enemy and Mother of my Enemy,' said the Cat, 'it is I: for you have spoken a word in my praise, and now I can sit within the Cave for always and always and always. But still I am the Cat who walks by himself, and all places are alike to me.'

The Woman was very angry, and shut her lips tight and took up her spinning-wheel and began to spin.

But the Baby cried because the Cat had gone away, and the Woman could not hush it, for it struggled and kicked and grew black in the face.

'O my Enemy and Wife of my Enemy and Mother of my Enemy,' said the Cat, 'take a strand of the thread that you are spinning and tie it to your spindle-whorl and drag it along the floor, and I will show you a Magic that shall make your Baby laugh as loudly as he is now crying.'

'I will do so,' said the Woman, 'because I am at my wits' end; but I will not thank you for it.'

She tied the thread to the little clay spindle-whorl and drew it across the floor, and the Cat ran after it and patted it with his paws and rolled head over heels, and tossed it backward over his shoulder and chased it between his hind legs and pretended to lose it, and pounced down upon it again, till the Baby laughed as loudly as it had been crying, and scrambled after the Cat and frolicked all over the Cave till it grew tired and settled down to sleep with the Cat in its arms.

'Now,' said the Cat, 'I will sing the Baby a song that shall keep him asleep for an hour.' And he began to purr, loud and low, low and loud, till the Baby fell fast asleep. The Woman smiled as she looked down upon the two of them, and said, 'That was wonderfully done. No question but you are very clever, O Cat.'

That very minute and second, Best Beloved, the smoke of the Fire at the back of the Cave came down in clouds from the roof – *puff!* – because it remembered the bargain she had made with the Cat; and when it had cleared away – lo and behold! – the Cat was sitting quite comfy close to the fire.

'O my Enemy and Wife of my Enemy and Mother to my Enemy,' said the Cat, 'it is I: for you have spoken a second word in my praise, and now I can sit by the warm fire at the back of the Cave for always and always and always. But still I am the Cat who walks by himself, and all places are alike to me.'

Then the woman was very very angry, and let down

her hair and put more wood on the fire and brought out the broad blade-bone of the shoulder of mutton and began to make a Magic that should prevent her from saying a third word in praise of the Cat. It was not a Singing Magic, Best Beloved, it was a Still Magic; and by and by the Cave grew so still that a little wee-wee mouse crept out of a corner and ran across the floor.

'O my Enemy and Wife of my Enemy and Mother of my Enemy,' said the Cat, 'is that little mouse part of your Magic?'

'Ouh! Chee! No indeed!' said the Woman, and she dropped the blade-bone and jumped upon the footstool in front of the fire and braided up her hair quick for fear that the mouse should run up it.

'Ah,' said the Cat, watching. 'Then the mouse will do me no harm if I eat it?'

'No,' said the Woman, braiding up her hair, 'eat it quickly and I will ever be grateful to you.'

Cat made one jump and caught the little mouse and the Woman said, 'A hundred thanks. Even the First Friend is not quick enough to catch little mice as you have done. You must be very wise.'

That very minute and second, O Best Beloved, the Milk-pot that stood by the fire cracked in two pieces – *ffft!* – because it remembered the bargain she had made with the Cat; and when the Woman jumped down from the footstool – lo and behold! – the Cat was lapping up the warm white milk that lay in one of the broken pieces.

'O my Enemy and Wife of my Enemy and Mother of my Enemy,' said the Cat, 'it is I: for you have spoken three words in my praise, and now I can drink the warm white milk three times a day for always and always and always. But *still* I am the Cat who walks by himself, and all places are alike to me.'

Then the Woman laughed and set the Cat a bowl of the warm white milk and said, 'O Cat, you are as clever as a man, but remember that your bargain was not made with the Man or the Dog, and I do not know what they will do when they come home.'

'What is that to me?' said the Cat. 'If I have my place in the Cave by the fire and my warm white milk three times a day I do not care what the Man or the Dog can do.'

That evening when the Man and the Dog came into the Cave, the Woman told them all the story of the bargain, while the Cat sat by the fire amd smiled. Then the Man said, 'Yes, but he has not made a bargain with *me* or with all proper Men after me.' Then he took off his two leather boots and he took up his little stone axe (that makes three) and he fetched a piece of wood and a hatchet (that is five altogether), and he set them out in a row and he said, 'Now we will make *our* bargain. If you do not catch mice when you are in the Cave for always and always and always, I will throw these five things at you whenever I see you, and so shall all proper Men do after me.'

'Ah!' said the Woman, listening. 'That is a very clever Cat, but he is not so clever as my Man.'

The Cat counted the five things (and they looked very knobby) and he said, 'I will catch mice when I am in the Cave for always and always and always; but *still* I am the Cat who walks by himself, and all places are alike to me.'

'Not when I am near,' said the Man. 'If you had not said that last I would have put all these things away for always and always and always; but now I am going to throw my two boots and my little stone axe (that makes three) at you whenever I meet you. And so shall all proper Men do after me!'

Then the Dog said, 'Wait a minute. He has not made a bargain with *me* or with all proper Dogs after me.' And he showed his teeth and said, 'If you are not kind to the Baby while I am in the Cave for always and always and always, I will hunt you till I catch you, and when I catch you I will bite you. And so shall all proper Dogs do after me.'

'Ah!' said the Woman, listening. 'This is a very clever Cat, but he is not so clever as the Dog.'

Cat counted the Dog's teeth (and they looked very pointed) and he said, 'I will be kind to the Baby while I am in the Cave, as long as he does not pull my tail too hard, for always and always and always. But *still* I am the Cat who walks by himself, and all places are alike to me.'

'Not when I am near,' said the Dog. 'If you had not said that last I would have shut my mouth for always and always and always; but *now* I am going to hunt you up a tree whenever I meet you. And so shall all proper Dogs do after me.'

Then the Man threw his two boots and his little stone axe (that makes three) at the Cat, and the Cat ran out of the Cave and the Dog chased him up a tree; and from that day to this, Best Beloved, three proper Men out of five will always throw things at a Cat whenever they meet him, and all proper Dogs will chase him up a tree. But the Cat keeps his side of the bargain too. He will kill mice, and he will be kind to Babies when he is in the house, just as long as they do not pull his tail too hard. But when he has done that, and between times, and when the moon gets up and night comes, he is the Cat that walks by himself, and all places are alike to him. Then he goes out to the Wet Wild Woods or up the Wet Wild Trees or on the Wet Wild Roofs, waving his wild tail and walking by his wild lone.

The Boy Who Talked With Animals

from *The Wonderful Story of Henry Sugar* by Roald Dahl

NOT so long ago, I decided to spend a few days in the West Indies. I was to go there for a short holiday. Friends had told me it was marvellous. I would laze around all day, they said, sunning myself on the silver beaches and swimming in the warm green sea.

I chose Jamaica, and flew direct from London to Kingston. The drive from Kingston airport to my hotel on the north shore took two hours. The island was full of mountains and the mountains were covered all over with dark tangled forests. The big Jamaican who drove the taxi told me that up in those forests lived whole communities of diabolical people who still practised voodoo and witch-doctory and other magic rites. 'Don't ever go up into those mountain forests,' he said, rolling his eyes. 'There's things happening up there that'd make your hair turn white in a minute!'

'What sort of things?' I asked him.

'It's better you don't ask,' he said. 'It don't pay even to talk about it.' And that was all he would say on the subject.

My hotel lay upon the edge of a pearly beach, and the setting was even more beautiful than I had imagined. But the moment I walked in through those big open front doors, I began to feel uneasy. There was no reason for this. I couldn't see anything wrong. But the feeling was there and I couldn't shake it off. There was something weird and sinister about the place. Despite all the loveliness and the luxury, there was a whiff of danger that hung and drifted in the air like poisonous gas.

And I wasn't sure it was just the hotel. The whole island, the mountains and the forests, the black rocks along the coastline and the trees cascading with brilliant scarlet flowers, all these and many other things made me feel uncomfortable in my skin. There was something malignant crouching underneath the surface of this island. I could sense it in my bones.

My room in the hotel had a little balcony, and from there I could step straight down on to the beach. There were tall coconut palms growing all around, and every so often an enormous green nut the size of a football would fall out of the sky and drop with a thud on the sand. It was considered foolish to linger underneath a coconut palm because if one of those things landed on your head, it would smash your skull.

The Jamaican girl who came in to tidy my room told me that a wealthy American called Mr Wasserman had met his end in precisely this manner only two months before.

'You're joking,' I said to her.

'Not joking!' she cried. 'No *suh*! I sees it happening with my very own eyes!'

'But wasn't there a terrific fuss about it?' I asked.

'They hush it up,' she answered darkly. 'The hotel folks hush it up and so do the newspaper folks because things like that are very bad for the tourist business.'

'And you say you actually saw it happen?'

'I actually saw it happen,' she said. 'Mr Wasserman,

he's standing right under that very tree over there on the beach. He's got his camera out and he's pointing it at the sunset. It's a red sunset that evening, and very pretty. Then all at once, down comes a big green nut right smack on to the top of his bald-head. *Wham!* And that,' she added with a touch of relish, ' is the very last sunset Mr Wasserman ever did see.'

'You mean it killed him instantly?'

'I don't know about *instantly*,' she said. 'I remember the next thing that happens is the camera falls out of his hands on to the sand. Then his arms drop down to his sides and hang there. Then he starts swaying. He sways backwards and forwards several times ever so gentle, and I'm standing there watching him, and I says to myself the poor man's gone all dizzy and maybe he's going to faint any moment. Then very very slowly he keels right over and down he goes.'

'Was he dead?'

'Dead as a doornail,' she said.

'Good heavens.'

'That's right,' she said. 'It never pays to be standing under a coconut palm when there's a breeze blowing.'

'Thank you,' I said. 'I'll remember that.'

On the evening of my second day, I was sitting on my little balcony with a book on my lap and a tall glass of rum punch in my hand. I wasn't reading the book. I was watching a small green lizard stalking another small green lizard on the balcony floor about six feet away. The stalking lizard was coming up on the other one from behind, moving forward very slowly and very cautiously, and when he came within reach, he flicked out a long tongue and touched the other one's tail. The other one jumped round, and the two of them faced each other, motionless, glued to the floor, crouching, staring and very tense. Then suddenly, they started doing a funny little hopping dance together. They hopped up in the air. They hopped backwards.

They hopped forwards. They hopped sideways. They circled one another like two boxers, hopping and prancing and dancing all the time. It was a queer thing to watch, and I guessed it was some sort of a courtship ritual they were going through. I kept very still, waiting to see what was going to happen next.

But I never saw what happened next because at that moment I became aware of a great commotion on the beach below. I glanced over and saw a crowd of people clustering around something at the water's edge. There was a narrow canoe-type fisherman's boat pulled up on the sand near by, and all I could think of was that the fisherman had come in with a lot of fish and that the crowd was looking at it.

A haul of fish is something that has always fascinated me. I put my book aside and stood up. More people were trooping down from the hotel veranda and hurrying over the beach to join the crowd on the edge of the water. The men were wearing those frightful Bermuda shorts that come down to the knees, and their shirts were bilious with pinks and oranges and every other clashing colour you could think of. The women had better taste, and were dressed for the most part in pretty cotton dresses. Nearly everyone carried a drink in one hand.

I picked up my own drink and stepped down from the balcony on to the beach. I made a little detour around the coconut palm under which Mr Wasserman had supposedly met his end, and strode across the beautiful silvery sand to join the crowd.

But it wasn't a haul of fish they were staring at. It was a turtle, an upside-down turtle lying on its back in the sand. But what a turtle it was! It was a giant, a mammoth. I had not thought it possible for a turtle to be as enormous as this. How can I describe its size? Had it been the right way up, I think a tall man could have sat on its back without his feet touching the ground. It was perhaps five feet long and four feet across with a high domed shell of great beauty.

The fisherman who had caught it had tipped it on its back to stop it from getting away. There was also a thick rope tied around the middle of its shell, and one proud fisherman, slim and black and naked except for a small loincloth, stood a short way off holding the end of the rope with both hands.

Upside down it lay, this magnificent creature, with its four thick flippers waving frantically in the air, and its long wrinkled neck stretching far out of its shell. The flippers had large sharp claws on them.

'Stand back, ladies and gentlemen, please!' cried the fisherman. 'Stand well back! Them claws is *dangerous*, man! They'll rip your arm clear away from your body!'

The crowd of hotel guests was thrilled and delighted by this spectacle. A dozen cameras were out and clicking away. Many of the women were squealing with pleasure and clutching on to the arms of their men, and the men were demonstrating their lack of fear and their masculinity by making foolish remarks in loud voices.

'Make yourself a nice pair of horn-rimmed spectacles out of that shell, hey Al?'

'Darn thing must weigh over a ton!'

'You mean to say it can actually float?'

'Sure it floats. Powerful swimmer, too. Pull a boat easy.'

'He's a snapper, is he?'

'That's no snapper. Snapper turtles don't grow as big as that. But I'll tell you what. He'll snap your hand off quick enough if you get too close to him.'

'Is that true?' one of the women asked the fisherman. 'Would he snap off a person's hand?'

'He would right now,' the fisherman said, smiling with brilliant white teeth. 'He won't ever hurt you when he's in the ocean, but you catch him and pull him ashore and tip him up like this, then man alive, you'd better watch out! He'll snap at anything that comes in reach!'

'I guess I'd get a bit snappish myself,' the woman said, 'if I was in his situation.'

One idiotic man had found a plank of driftwood on the sand, and he was carrying it toward the turtle. It was a fair-sized plank, about five feet long and maybe an inch thick. He started poking one end of it at the turtle's head.

'I wouldn't do that,' the fisherman said. 'You'll only make him madder than ever.'

When the end of the plank touched the turtle's neck, the great head whipped round and the mouth opened wide and *snap*, it took the plank in its mouth and bit through it as if it were made of cheese.

'Wow!' they shouted. 'Did you see that! I'm glad it wasn't my arm!'

'Leave him alone,' the fisherman said. 'It don't help to get him all stirred up.'

A paunchy man with wide hips and very short legs came up to the fisherman and said, 'Listen, feller. I want that shell. I'll buy it from you.' And to his plump wife, he said, 'You know what I'm going to do, Mildred? I'm going to take that shell home and have it polished up by an expert. Then I'm going to place it smack in the centre of our living-room! Won't that be something?'

'Fantastic,' the plump wife said. 'Go ahead and buy it, baby.'

'Don't worry,' he said. 'It's mine already.' And to the fisherman, he said, 'How much for the shell?'

'I already sold him,' the fisherman said. 'I sold him shell and all.'

'Not so fast, feller,' the paunchy man said. 'I'll bid you higher. Come on. What'd he offer you?'

'No can do,' the fisherman said. 'I already sold him.'

'Who to?' the paunchy man said.

'To the manager.'

'What manager?'

'The manager of the hotel.'

'Did you hear that?' shouted another man. 'He's sold it to the manager of our hotel! And you know what that means? It means turtle soup, that's what it means!'

'Right you are! And turtle steak! You ever have a turtle steak, Bill?'

'I never have, Jack. But I can't wait.'

'A turtle steak's better than a beefsteak if you cook it right. It's more tender and it's got one heck of a flavour.'

'Listen,' the paunchy man said to the fisherman. 'I'm not trying to buy the meat. The manager can have the meat. He can have everything that's inside including the teeth and toe nails. All I want is the shell.'

'And if I know you, baby,' his wife said, beaming at him, 'you're going to get the shell.'

I stood there listening to the conversation of these human beings. They were discussing the destruction, the consumption and the flavour of a creature who seemed, even when upside down, to be extraordinarily dignified. One thing was certain. He was senior to any of them in age. For probably one hundred and fifty years he had been cruising in the green waters of the West Indies. He was there when George Washington was President of the United States and Napoleon was being clobbered at Waterloo. He would have been a small turtle then, but he was most certainly there.

And now he was here, upside down on the beach, waiting to be sacrificed for soup and steak. He was clearly alarmed by all the noise and shouting around him. His old wrinkled neck was straining out of its shell, and the great head was twisting this way and that as though searching for someone who would explain the reason for all this ill-treatment.

'How are you going to get him up to the hotel?' the paunchy man asked.

'Drag him up the beach with the rope,' the fisherman answered. 'The staff'll be coming along soon to take him. It's going to need ten men, all pulling at once.'

'Hey, listen!' cried a muscular young man. 'Why don't *we* drag him up?' The muscular young man was wearing magenta and pea-green Bermuda shorts and no shirt. He had an exceptionally hairy chest, and the absence of a shirt was obviously a calculated touch. 'What say we do a little work for our supper?' he cried, rippling his muscles. 'Come on, fellers! Who's for some exercise?'

'Great idea!' they shouted. 'Splendid scheme!'

The men handed their drinks to the women and rushed to catch hold of the rope. They ranged themselves along it as though for a tug of war, and the hairy-chested man appointed himself anchor-man and captain of the team.

'Come on, now, fellers!' he shouted. 'When I say *heave*, then all heave at once, you understand?'

The fisherman didn't like this much. 'It's better you leave this job for the hotel,' he said.

'Rubbish!' shouted hairy-chest. '*Heave*, boys, heave!'

They all heaved. The gigantic turtle wobbled on its back and nearly toppled over.

'Don't tip him!' yelled the fisherman. 'You're going to tip him over if you do that! And if he once gets back on to his legs again, he'll escape for sure!'

'Cool it, laddie,' said hairy-chest in a patronizing voice. 'How can he escape? We've got a rope round him, haven't we?'

'That old turtle will drag the whole lot of you away with him if you give him a chance!' cried the fisherman. 'He'll drag you out into the ocean, every one of you!'

'*Heave*!' shouted hairy-chest, ignoring the fisherman. '*Heave*, boys, *heave*!'

And now the gigantic turtle began very slowly to slide up the beach toward the hotel, toward the kitchen, toward the place where the big knives were kept. The womenfolk and the older, fatter, less athletic men followed alongside, shouting encouragement.

'*Heave*!' shouted the hairy-chested anchor-man. 'Put your backs into it, fellers! You can pull harder than that!'

Suddenly, I heard screams. Everyone heard them. They were screams so high-pitched, so shrill and so urgent they cut right through everything. 'No-o-o-o-o!' screamed the scream. 'No! No! No! No! No!'

The crowd froze. The tug of war men stopped tugging and the onlookers stopped shouting and every single person present turned towards the place where the screams were coming from.

Half walking, half running down the beach from the hotel, I saw three people, a man, a woman and a small boy. They were half running because the boy was pulling the man along. The man had the boy by the wrist, trying to slow him down, but the boy kept pulling. At the same time, he was jumping and twisting and wriggling and trying to free himself from the father's grip. It was the boy who was screaming.

'Don't!' he screamed. 'Don't do it! Let him go! Please let him go!'

The woman, his mother, was trying to catch hold of the boy's other arm to help restrain him, but the boy was jumping about so much, she didn't succeed.

'Let him go!' screamed the boy. 'It's horrible what you're doing! Please let him go!'

'Stop that, David!' the mother said, still trying to catch his other arm. 'Don't be childish! You're making a perfect fool of yourself.'

'Daddy!' the boy screamed. 'Daddy! Tell them to let him go!'

'I can't do that, David,' the father said. 'It isn't any of our business.'

The tug of war pullers remained motionless, still holding the rope with the gigantic turtle on the end of it. Everyone stood silent and surprised, staring at the boy. They were all a bit off balance now. They had the slightly hangdog air of people who had been caught doing something that was not entirely honourable.

'Come on now, David,' the father said, pulling against the boy. 'Let's go back to the hotel and leave these people alone.'

'I'm not going back!' the boy shouted. 'I don't want to go back! I want them to let it go!'

'Now, David,' the mother said.

'Beat it, kid,' the hairy-chested man told the boy.

'You're horrible and cruel!' the boy shouted. 'All of you are horrible and cruel!' He threw the words high and shrill at the forty or fifty adults standing there on the beach, and nobody, not even the hairy-chested man, answered him this time. 'Why don't you put him back in the sea?' the boy shouted. 'He hasn't done anything to you! Let him go!'

The father was embarrassed by his son, but he was not ashamed of him. 'He's crazy about animals,' he said, addressing the crowd. 'Back home he's got every kind of animal under the sun. He talks with them.'

'He loves them,' the mother said.

Several people began shuffling their feet around in the sand. Here and there in the crowd it was possible to sense a slight change of mood, a feeling of uneasiness, a touch even of shame. The boy, who could have been no more than eight or nine years old, had stopped struggling with his father now. The father still held him by the wrist, but he was no longer restraining him.

'Go on!' the boy called out. 'Let him go! Undo the rope and let him go!' He stood very small and erect, facing the crowd, his eyes shining like two stars and the wind blowing in his hair. He was magnificent.

'There's nothing we can do, David,' the father said gently. 'Let's go on back.'

'No!' the boy cried out, and at that moment he suddenly gave a twist and wrenched his wrist free from the father's grip. He was away like a streak, running across the sand toward the giant upturned turtle.

'David!' the father yelled, starting after him. 'Stop! Come back!'

The boy dodged and swerved through the crowd like a player running with the ball, and the only person who sprang forward to intercept him was the fisherman. 'Don't you go near that turtle, boy!' he shouted as he made a lunge for the swiftly running figure. But the boy dodged round him and kept going. 'He'll bite you to pieces!' yelled the fisherman. 'Stop, boy! Stop!'

But it was too late to stop him now, and as he came running straight at the turtle's head, the turtle saw him, and the huge upside-down head turned quickly to face him.

The voice of the boy's mother, the stricken, agonized wail of the mother's voice rose up into the evening sky. 'David!' it cried. '*Oh, David!*' And a moment later, the boy was throwing himself on to his knees in the sand and flinging his arms around the wrinkled old neck and hugging the creature to his chest. The boy's cheek was pressing against the turtle's head, and his lips were moving, whispering soft words that nobody else could hear. The turtle became absolutely still. Even the giant flippers stopped waving in the air.

A great sigh, a long soft sigh of relief, went up from the crowd. Many people took a pace or two backward, as though trying perhaps to get a little further away from something that was beyond their understanding. But the father and mother came forward together and stood about ten feet away from their son.

'Daddy!' the boy cried out, still caressing the old brown head. 'Please do something, Daddy! Please make them let him go!'

'Can I be of any help here?' said a man in a white suit who had just come down from the hotel. This, as everyone knew, was Mr Edwards, the manager. He was a tall, beak-nosed Englishman with a long pink face. '*What*

*And a moment later, the boy was throwing himself on his knees in the sand
and flinging his arms around the wrinkled old neck*

an extraordinary thing!' he said, looking at the boy and
the turtle. 'He's lucky he hasn't had his head bitten off.'
And to the boy he said, 'You'd better come away from
there now, sonny. That thing's dangerous.'

'I want them to let him go!' cried the boy, still cradling
the head in his arms. 'Tell them to let him go!'

'You realize he could be killed any moment,' the
manager said to the boy's father.

'Leave him alone,' the father said.

'Rubbish,' the manager said. 'Go in and grab him. But
be quick. And be careful.'

'No,' the father said.

'What do you mean, no?' said the manager. 'These
things are lethal! Don't you understand that?'

'Yes,' the father said.

'Then for heaven's sake, man, get him away!' cried the manager. 'There's going to be a very nasty accident if you don't.'

'Who owns it?' the father said. 'Who owns the turtle?'

'We do,' the manager said. 'The hotel has bought it.'

'Then do me a favour,' the father said. 'Let me buy it from you.'

The manager looked at the father, but said nothing.

'You don't know my son,' the father said, speaking quietly. 'He'll go crazy if it's taken up to the hotel and slaughtered. He'll become hysterical.'

'Just pull him away,' the manager said. 'And be quick about it.'

'He loves animals,' the father said. 'He really loves them. He communicates with them.

The crowd was silent, trying to hear what was being said. Nobody moved away. They stood as though hypnotized.

'If we let it go,' the manager said, 'they'll only catch it again.'

'Perhaps they will,' the father said. 'But those things can swim.'

'I know they can swim,' the manager said. 'They'll catch him all the same. This is a valuable item, you must realize that. The shell alone is worth a lot of money.'

'I don't care about the cost,' the father said. 'Don't worry about that. I want to buy it.'

The boy was still kneeling in the sand beside the turtle, caressing its head.

The manager took a handkerchief from his breast pocket and started wiping his fingers. He was not keen to let the turtle go. He probably had the dinner menu already planned. On the other hand, he didn't want another gruesome accident on his private beach this season. Mr Wasserman and the coconut, he told himself, had been quite enough for one year, thank you very much.

The father said, 'I would deem it a great personal favour, Mr Edwards, if you would let me buy it. And I promise you won't regret it. I'll make quite sure of that.'

The manager's eyebrows went up just a fraction of an inch. He had got the point. He was being offered a bribe. That was a different matter. For a few seconds he went on wiping his hands with the handkerchief. Then he shrugged his shoulders and said, 'Well, I suppose if it will make your boy feel any better . . .'

'Thank you,' the father said.

'Oh, thank you!' the mother cried. 'Thank you so very much!'

'Willy,' the manager said, beckoning to the fisherman.

The fisherman came forward. He looked thoroughly confused. 'I never seen anything like this before in my whole life,' he said. 'This old turtle was the fiercest I ever caught! He fought like a devil when we brought him in! It took all six of us to land him! That boy's crazy!'

'Yes, I know,' the manager said. 'But now I want you to let him go.'

'Let him go!' the fisherman cried, aghast. 'You mustn't ever let this one go, Mr Edwards! He's broke the record! He's the biggest turtle ever been caught on this island! Easy the biggest! And what about our money?'

'You'll get your money.'

'I got the other five to pay off as well,' the fisherman said, pointing down the beach.

About a hundred yards down, on the water's edge, five black skinned almost naked men were standing beside a second boat. 'All six of us are in on this, equal shares,' the fisherman went on. 'I can't let him go till we got the money.'

'I guarantee you'll get it,' the manager said. 'Isn't that good enough for you?'

'I'll underwrite that guarantee,' the father of the boy said, stepping forward. 'And there'll be an extra bonus for all six of the fishermen just as long as you let him go at once. I mean immediately, this instant.'

The fisherman looked at the father. Then he looked at the manager. 'Okay,' he said. 'If that's the way you want it.'

'There's one condition,' the father said. 'Before you get your money, you must promise you won't go straight out and try to catch him again. Not this evening, anyway. Is that understood?'

'Sure,' the fisherman said. 'That's a deal.' He turned and ran down the beach, calling to the other five fishermen. He shouted something to them that we couldn't hear, and in a minute or two, all six of them came back together. Five of them were carrying long thick wooden poles.

The boy was still kneeling beside the turtle's head. 'David,' the father said to him gently. 'It's all right now, David. They're going to let him go.'

The boy looked round, but he didn't take his arms from around the turtle's neck, and he didn't get up. 'When?' he asked.

'Now,' the father said. 'Right now. So you'd better come away.'

'You promise?' the boy said.

'Yes, David, I promise.'

The boy withdrew his arms. He got to his feet. He stepped back a few paces.

'Stand back everyone!' shouted the fisherman called Willy. 'Stand right back everybody, please!'

The crowd moved a few yards up the beach. The tug of war men let go the rope and moved back with the others.

Willy got down on his hands and knees and crept very cautiously up to one side of the turtle. Then he began untying the knot in the rope. He kept well out of the range of the big flippers as he did this.

When the knot was untied, Willy crawled back. Then the five other fishermen stepped forward with their poles. The poles were about seven feet long and immensely thick. They wedged them underneath the shell of the turtle and began to rock the great creature from side to side on its shell. The shell had a high dome and was well shaped for rocking.

'Up and down!' sang the fishermen as they rocked away. 'Up and down! Up and down! Up and down!' The old turtle became thoroughly upset, and who could blame it? The big flippers lashed the air frantically, and the head kept shooting in and out of the shell.

'Roll him over!' sang the fishermen. 'Up and over! Roll him over! One more time and over he goes!'

The turtle tilted high up on to its side and crashed down in the sand the right way up.

But it didn't walk away at once. The huge brown head came out and peered cautiously around.

'Go, turtle, go!' the small boy called out. 'Go back to the sea!'

The two hooded black eyes of the turtle peered up at the boy. The eyes were bright and lively, full of the wisdom of great age. The boy looked back at the turtle, and this time when he spoke, his voice was soft and intimate. 'Good-bye, old man,' he said. 'Go far away this time.' The black eyes remained resting on the boy for a few seconds more. Nobody moved. Then, with great dignity, the massive beast turned away and began waddling toward the edge of the ocean. He didn't hurry. He moved sedately over the sandy beach, the big shell rocking gently from side to side as he went.

The crowd watched in silence.

He entered the water.

He kept going.

Soon he was swimming. He was in his element now. He swam gracefully and very fast, with the head held high. The sea was calm, and he made little waves that fanned out behind him on both sides, like the waves of a boat. It was several minutes before we lost sight of him, and by then he was half-way to the horizon.

The guests began wandering back toward the hotel. They were curiously subdued. There was no joking or bantering now, no laughing. Something had happened. Something strange had come fluttering across the beach.

I walked back to my small balcony and sat down with a cigarette. I had an uneasy feeling that this was not the end of the affair.

The next morning at eight o'clock, the Jamaican girl, the one who had told me about Mr Wasserman and the coconut, brought a glass of orange juice to my room.

'Big *big* fuss in the hotel this morning,' she said as she placed the glass on the table and drew back the curtains. 'Everyone flying about all over the place like they was crazy.'

'Why? What's happened?'

'That little boy in number twelve, he's vanished. He disappeared in the night.'

'You mean the turtle boy?'

'That's him,' she said. 'His parents is raising the roof and the manager's going mad.'

'How long's he been missing?'

'About two hours ago his father found his bed empty. But he could've gone any time in the night I reckon.'

'Yes,' I said. 'He could.'

'Everybody in the hotel searching high and low,' she said. 'And a police car just arrived.'

'Maybe he just got up early and went for a climb on the rocks,' I said.

Her large dark haunted-looking eyes rested for a moment on my face, then travelled away. 'I do not think so,' she said, and out she went.

I slipped on some clothes and hurried down to the beach. On the beach itself, two native policemen in khaki uniforms were standing with Mr Edwards, the manager. Mr Edwards was doing the talking. The policemen were listening patiently. In the distance, at both ends of the beach, I could see small groups of people, hotel servants as well as hotel guests, spreading out and heading for the rocks. The morning was beautiful. The sky was smoke blue, faintly glazed with yellow. The sun was up and making diamonds all over the smooth sea. And Mr Edwards was talking loudly to the two native policemen, and waving his arms.

I wanted to help. What should I do? Which way should I go? It would be pointless simply to follow the others. So I just kept walking toward Mr Edwards.

About then, I saw the fishing-boat. The long wooden canoe with a single mast and a flapping brown sail was still some way out to sea, but it was heading for the beach. The two natives aboard, one at either end, were paddling hard. They were paddling very hard. The paddles rose and fell at such a terrific speed they might have been in a race. I stopped and watched them. Why the great rush to the shore? Quite obviously they had something to tell. I kept my eyes on the boat. Over to my left, I could hear Mr Edwards saying to the two police-men, 'It is perfectly ridiculous. I can't have people disappearing just like that from the hotel. You'd better find him fast, you understand me? He's either wandered off somewhere and got lost or he's been kidnapped. Either way, it's the responsibility of the police . . .'

The fishing-boat skimmed over the sea and came gliding up on to the sand at the water's edge. Both men dropped their paddles and jumped out. They started running up the beach. I recognized the one in front as Willy. When he caught sight of the manager and the two policemen, he made straight for them.

'Hey, Mr Edwards!' Willy called out. 'We just seen a crazy thing!'

The manager stiffened and jerked back his neck. The two policemen remained impassive. They were used to excitable people. They met them every day.

Willy stopped in front of the group, his chest heaving

in and out with heavy breathing. The other fisherman was close behind him. They were both naked except for a tiny loincloth, their black skins shining with sweat.

'We been paddling full speed for a long way,' Willy said, excusing his out-of-breathness. 'We thought we ought to come back and tell it as quick as we can.'

'Tell what?' the manager said. 'What did you see?'

'It was crazy, man! Absolutely crazy!'

'Get on with it, Willy, for heaven's sake.'

'You won't believe it,' Willy said. 'There ain't nobody going to believe it. Isn't that right, Tom?'

'That's right,' the other fisherman said, nodding vigorously. 'If Willy here hadn't been with me to prove it, I wouldn't have believed it myself!'

'Believed what?' Mr Edwards said. 'Just tell us what you saw.'

'We'd gone off early,' Willy said, 'about four o'clock this morning, and we must've been a couple of miles out before it got light enough to see anything properly. Suddenly, as the sun comes up, we see right ahead of us, not more'n fifty yards away, we see something we couldn't believe not even with our own eyes . . .'

'What?' snapped Mr Edwards. 'For heaven's sake get on!'

'We sees that old monster turtle swimming away out there, the one on the beach yesterday, and we sees the boy sitting high up on the turtle's back and riding him over the sea like a horse!'

'You gotta believe it!' the other fisherman cried. 'I sees it too, so you gotta believe it!'

Mr Edwards looked at the two policemen. The two policemen looked at the fishermen. 'You wouldn't be having us on, would you?' one of the policemen said.

'I swear it!' cried Willy. 'It's the gospel truth! There's this little boy riding high up on the old turtle's back and his feet isn't even touching the water! He's dry as a bone and sitting there comfy and easy as could be! So we go after them. Of course we go after them. At first we try creeping up on them very quietly, like we always do when we're catching a turtle, but the boy sees us. We aren't very far away at this time, you understand. No more than from here to the edge of the water. And when the boy sees us, he sort of leans forward as if he's saying something to that old turtle, and the turtle's head comes up and he starts swimming like the clappers of hell! Man, could that turtle go! Tom and me can paddle pretty quick when we want to, but we've no chance against that monster! No chance at all! He's going at least twice as fast as we are! Easy twice as fast, what you say, Tom?'

'I'd say he's going *three times* as fast,' Tom said. 'And I'll tell you why. In about ten or fifteen minutes, they're a mile ahead of us.'

'Why on earth didn't you call out to the boy?' the manager asked. 'Why didn't you speak to him earlier on, when you were closer?'

'We never *stop* calling out, man!' Willy cried. 'As soon as the boy sees us and we're not trying to creep up on them any longer, then we start yelling. We yell everything under the sun at that boy to try and get him aboard. "Hey, boy!" I yell at him. "You come on back with us! We'll give you a lift home! That ain't no good what you're doing there, boy! Jump off and swim while you got the chance and we'll pick you up! Go on boy, jump! Your mammy must be waiting for you at home, boy, so why don't you come on in with us?" And once I shouted at him, "Listen, boy! We're gonna make you a promise! We promise not to catch that old turtle if you come with us!" '

'Did he answer you at all?' the manager asked.

'He never even looks round!' Willy said. 'He sits high up on that shell and he's sort of rocking backwards and forwards with his body just like he's urging the old turtle to go faster and faster! You're gonna lose that little boy,

171

Mr Edwards, unless someone gets out there real quick and grabs him away!'

The manager's normally pink face had turned white as paper. 'Which way were they heading?' he asked sharply.

'North,' Willy answered. 'Almost due north.'

'Right!' the manager said. 'We'll take the speed-boat! I want you with us, Willy. And you, Tom.'

The manager, the two policemen and the two fishermen ran down to where the boat that was used for water-skiing lay beached on the sand. They pushed the boat out, and even the manager lent a hand, wading up to his knees in his well-pressed white trousers. Then they all climbed in.

I watched them go zooming off.

Two hours later, I watched them coming back. They had seen nothing.

All through that day, speed-boats and yachts from other hotels along the coast searched the ocean. In the afternoon, the boy's father hired a helicopter. He rode in it himself and they were up there three hours. They found no trace of the turtle or the boy.

For a week, the search went on, but with no result.

And now, nearly a year has gone by since it happened. In that time, there has been only one significant bit of news. A party of Americans, out of Nassau in the Bahamas, were deep-sea fishing off a large island called Eleuthera. There are literally thousands of coral reefs and small uninhabited islands in this area, and upon one of these tiny islands, the captain of the yacht saw through his binoculars the figure of a small person. There was a sandy beach on the island, and the small person was walking on the beach. The binoculars were passed round, and everyone who looked through them agreed that it was a child of some sort. There was, of course, a lot of excitement on board and the fishing lines were quickly reeled in. The captain steered the yacht

172

straight for the island. When they were half a mile off, they were able, through the binoculars, to see clearly that the figure on the beach was a boy, and although sunburnt, he was almost certainly white-skinned, not a native. At that point, the watchers on the yacht also spotted what looked like a giant turtle on the sand near the boy. What happened next, happened very quickly. The boy, who had probably caught sight of the approaching yacht, jumped on to the turtle's back and the huge creature entered the water and swam at great speed around the island and out of sight. The yacht searched for two hours, but nothing more was seen either of the boy or the turtle.

There is no reason to disbelieve this report. There were five people on the yacht. Four of them were Americans and the captain was a Bahamian from Nassau. All of them in turn saw the boy and the turtle through the binoculars.

To reach Eleuthera Island from Jamaica by sea, one must first travel north-east for two hundred and fifty miles and pass through the Windward Passage between Cuba and Haiti. Then one must go north-west for a further three hundred miles at least. This is a total distance of five hundred and fifty miles, which is a very long journey for a small boy to make on the shell of a giant turtle.

Who knows what to think of all this?

One day, perhaps, he will come back, though I personally doubt it. I have a feeling he's quite happy where he is.

Christmas Eve

from *The Hundred and One Dalmatians* by Dodie Smith

The dogs are running away from the
wicked Cruella de Vil who wants to
have them killed so that she can have a
fur coat made from their skins. They
have tried to disguise their spots.

THEY had travelled about three miles when the first disaster of the night happened. There was a sudden bump, and a wild squeal from the Cadpig. A wheel had come off the little blue cart.

Pongo saw at once that the cart could be mended. A wooden peg which fixed the hub of the wheel to the axle had come out. But could he ever, using his teeth, put this peg back? He tried – and failed.

'Could the Cadpig manage without the cart?' he whispered to Missis.

Missis shook her head. Walking three fields had been enough for her smallest daughter. And her other daughters could not walk more than a mile without a rest.

'Then mend the cart I must,' said Pongo. 'And you must help me, by holding the wheel in position.'

They tried and tried, without success. Then, while they were resting for a moment, Missis noticed that many of the pups were shivering.

'They'd better keep warm by running races,' said Pongo.

'But that would tire them,' said Missis. 'Couldn't they all go to that barn over there?'

They could just see a big, tiled roof, two short fields away – not very clearly, because the moon was behind clouds; it was this lack of light which made it so hard to mend the cart.

'That's a good idea,' said Pongo. 'And when the cart's mended, we can bring it along and call for them all.'

Missis said the Cadpig had better stay in the cart and keep warm in the hay, but the Cadpig wanted to go with the others and see the barn – she felt sure she could walk two short fields. So Missis let her go. Two strong pups the right size to draw the cart stayed behind. They said they did not mind the cold.

So ninety-five pups, led by Lieutenant Lucky, set off briskly for the barn. But when they got there, it did not look at all like the barn at the Sheepdog's farm. It was built of grey stone and had long windows, some with coloured glass in them, and at one end was a tower.

'Why, there's a Folly!' said the Cadpig, remembering the tower of the Folly at Hell Hall.

Lucky was looking for a door, but when he found one it was firmly shut. He told the pups to wait for him, while he went round the building looking for some other way in.

The Cadpig did not wait. 'Come on,' she said to her devoted brother, Patch. 'I want to look at that Folly.'

And when they got to the tower, they saw a narrow door that was not quite closed. It was too heavy for them to push but they could – just . . . squeeze through.

Inside, this tower was nothing like the one at Hell Hall. And it opened into the grey stone building.

'No hay in this barn,' said the Cadpig.

She had counted on the hay for warmth, but she soon found she was warm enough without it, for there was a big stove alight. It had a long iron pipe for a chimney which went right up through the raftered ceiling. The

moon was out again now and its light was streaming in through the tall windows, so that the clear glass made silver patterns on the stone floor and the coloured glass made blue, gold and rose patterns. The Cadpig patted one of the coloured patterns with a delicate paw.

'I love this barn,' she said.

Patch said: 'I don't think it *is* a barn.' But he liked it as much as the Cadpig did.

They wandered around – and suddenly they made a discovery. Whatever this mysterious place was, it was certainly intended for puppies. For in front of every seat – and there were many seats – was a puppy-sized dog-bed, padded and most comfortable.

'Why, it's just *meant* for us all to sleep in!' said the Cadpig.

'I'll tell the other pups,' said Patch, starting for the door. A glad cry from the Cadpig called him back.

'Look, look! Television!'

But it was not like the Television at Hell Hall. It was much larger. And the figures on the screen did not move or speak. Indeed, it was not a screen. The figures were really there, on a low platform, humans and animals, most life-like, though smaller than in real life.

They were in a stable, above which was one bright star.

'Look at the little humans, kneeling,' said Patch.

'And there's a kind of a cow,' said the Cadpig, remembering the cows at the farm, who had given all the pups milk.

'And a kind of horse,' said Patch, remembering the helpful horses who had let them all out of the field.

'No dogs,' said the Cadpig. 'What a pity! But I like it much better than ordinary Television. Only I don't know why.'

Then they heard Lucky and the others, who had found their way in. Soon every pup was curled up on a comfortable dogbed and fast asleep – except the Cadpig. She had dragged along one of the dogbeds by its most convenient little carpet ear, and was sitting on it, wide awake, gazing and gazing at this new and far more beautiful Television.

Once the moon came out from behind the clouds Pongo managed to mend the wheel – oh, the feeling of satisfaction when the peg slipped into place! Missis, too, felt proud. Had she not *held* the wheel? She, a dog who had never understood machinery! Quickly the two waiting pups seized the cross-bar in their mouths. Then off they all went to the barn.

But as they drew nearer, Pongo saw this was no barn.

'Surely they can't have gone in *there*?' he said to Missis.

'Why not, if they were cold?' said Missis. 'And they are far too young to know they would not be welcome.'

Pongo and Missis both knew that humans did not like dogs to go into buildings which had towers and tall, narrow windows. They had no idea why, and had at first been a little hurt when told firmly to wait outside. But Mrs. Dearly had once said: 'We would love you to come in if it was allowed. And *I* would go in far oftener if *you* could.' So it was obviously one of those mysterious things such as no one – not even humans – ever being allowed to walk on certain parts of the grass in Regent's Park.

'We must get them out quickly,' said Pongo, 'and go on with our journey.'

They soon found the door in the tower – which the biggest pups had pushed wide open. Because Missis had always been left outside, she disliked these curious buildings with towers and high windows; but the minute she got inside, she changed her mind. This was a wonderful place – so peaceful and, somehow, so welcoming.

'But where are the pups?' she said, peering all around.

She saw lots of black patches on the moonlit floor but had quite forgotten that all the pups were now black. Then she remembered and as she drew nearer to the sleeping pups, tears sprang to her eyes.

'Look, look at all the puppybeds!' she cried. 'What *good* people must live here!'

'It can't be the kind of place I thought it was,' said Pongo.

He was about to wake the puppies when Missis stopped him.

'Let me sit by the stove for a little while,' she said.

'Not too long, my dear,' said Pongo.

He need not have worried. Missis only sat still for a few minutes. Then she got up, shook herself, and said brightly:

'Let us start now. Things are going to be all right.'

An hour or so later, just before the evening service, the Verger said to the Vicar:

'I think there must be something wrong with the stove, sir.'

On every hassock he had found a small, circular patch of soot.

An Otter Hunt

from *Tarka the Otter*
by Henry Williamson

H E was awakened by the tremendous baying of
hounds. He saw feet splashing in the shallow
water, a row of noses and many flacking tongues.
The entrance was too small for any head to enter.
He crawled a yard away, against the cold rock. The noise
hurt the fine drums of his ears.

Hob-nailed boots scraped on the brown shillets of the
waterbed, and iron-tipped hunting poles tapped the
rocks.

Go'r'n leave it! Leave it! Go'r'n leave it! Deadlock! Harper!
Go'r'n leave it!

Tarka heard the horn and the low opening became
lighter.

Go'r'n leave it! Captain! Deadlock! Go'r'n leave it!

The horn twanged fainter as the pack was taken away.
Then a pole was thrust into the hole and prodded about
blindly. It slid out again. Tarka saw boots and hands and
the face of a terrier. A voice whispered, *Leu in there,*
Sammy, leu in there! The small ragged brown animal crept
out of the hands. Sammy smelled Tarka, saw him, and

began to sidle towards him. *Waugh-waugh-waugh-wa-waugh.* As the otter did not move, the terrier crept nearer to him, yapping with head stretched forward.

After a minute Tarka could bear the irritating noises no more. Hissing, with open mouth, he moved past the terrier, whose snarly yapping changed to a high-pitched yelping. The men on the opposite bank stood silent and still. They saw Tarka's head in sunlight, which came through the trees behind them and turned the brown shillets a warm yellow. The water ran clear and cold. Tarka saw three men in blue coats; they did not move, and he slipped into the water. It did not cover his back, and he returned to the bankside roots. He moved in the shadows and under the ferns at his ordinary travelling pace. One of three watching men declared that an otter had no sense of fear.

No hound spoke, but the reason of the silence was not considered by Tarka, who could not reason such things. He had been awakened with a shock, he had been tormented by a noise, he had left a dangerous place, and he was escaping from human enemies. As he walked upstream, with raised head, his senses of smell, sight, and hearing were alert for his greatest enemies, the hounds.

The stream being narrow and shallow, the otter was given four minutes' law. Four minutes after Tarka had left he heard behind him the short and long notes of the horn, and the huntsman crying amidst the tongues of hounds, *Ol-ol-ol-ol-ol-over! Get on to'm! Ol-ol-ol-ol-over!* as the pack returned to full cry to the water. Hounds splashed into the water around the rock, wedging themselves at its opening and breaking into couples and half-couples, leaping through the water after the wet and shivering terrier, throwing their tongues and dipping their noses to the wash of scent coming down.

Deadlock plunged at the lead, with Coraline, Sailoress, Captain, and Playboy. They passed the terrier, and

Deadlock was so eager that he knocked him down. Sammy picked up his shivery body and followed.

Tarka sank all but his nostrils in a pool and waited. He lay in the sunlit water like a brown log slanting to the stones on which his rudder rested. The huntsman saw him. Tarka lifted his whiskered head out of the water and snarled at the huntsman. Hounds were speaking just below. From the pool the stream flowed for six feet down the smooth slide up which he had crept. When Deadlock jumped into the pool and lapped the scent lying on the water, Tarka put down his head with hardly a ripple, and like a skin of brown oil moved under the hound's belly. Soundlessly he emerged, and the sun glistened on his water-sleeked coat as he walked down on the algae-smeared rock. He seemed to walk under their muzzles slowly, and to be treading on their feet.

Let hounds hunt him! Don't help hounds or they'll chop him!

The pack was confused. Every hound owned the scent, which was like a tangled line, the end of which was sought for unravelling. But soon Deadlock pushed through the pack and told the way the otter had gone.

As Tarka was running over shillets, with water scarcely deep enough to cover his rudder, Deadlock saw him and with stiff stern ran straight at him. Tarka quitted the water. The dead twigs and leaves at the hedge-bottom crackled and rustled as he pushed through to the meadow. While he was running over the grass, he could hear the voice of Deadlock raging as the bigger black-and-white hound struggled through the hazel twigs and brambles and honeysuckle bines. He crossed fifty yards of meadow, climbed the bank, and ran down again on to a tarred road. The surface burned his pads, but he ran on, and even when an immense crimson creature bore down upon him he did not go back into the meadow across which hounds were streaming. With a series of shudders the crimson creature slowed to a standstill, while human figures rose out of it, and pointed. He ran under the motor-coach, and came out into brown sunshine, hearing above the shouts of men the clamour of hounds trying to scramble up the high bank and pulling each other down in their eagerness.

He ran in the shade of the ditch, among bits of newspaper, banana and orange skins, cigarette ends, and crushed chocolate boxes. A long yellow creature grew bigger and bigger before him, and women rose out of it and peered down at him as he passed it. With smarting eyes he ran two hundred yards of the road, which for him was a place of choking stinks and hurtful noises. Pausing in the ditch, he harkened to the clamour changing its tone as hounds leaped down into the road. He ran on for another two hundred yards, then climbed the bank, pushed through dusty leaves and grasses and briars that would hold him, and down the sloping meadow to the stream. He splashed into the water and swam until rocks and boulders rose before him. He climbed and walked over them. His rudder drawn on mosses and lichens left a strong scent behind him. Deadlock, racing over the green-shadowed grassland, threw his tongue before the pack.

In the water, through shallow and pool, his pace was steady, but not hurried; he moved faster than the stream; he insinuated himself from slide to pool, from pool to boulder, leaving his scent in the wet marks of his pads and rudder.

People were running through the meadow, and in the near distance arose the notes of the horn and hoarse cries. Hounds' tongues broke out united and firm, and Tarka knew that they had reached the stream. The sun-laden water of the pools was spun into eddies by the thrusts of his webbed hind-legs. He passed through shadow and dapple, through runnel and plash. The water sparkled amber in the sunbeams, and his brown sleek pelt glistened whenever his back made ripples. His movements in water were unhurried, like an eel's.

The hounds came nearer.

The stream after a bend flowed near the roadway, where more motor-cars were drawn up. Some men and women, holding notched poles, were watching from the cars – sportsmen on wheels.

Beggars' Roost Bridge was below. With hounds so near Tarka was heedless of the men that leaned over the stone parapet, watching for him. They shouted, waved hats, and cheered the hounds. There were ducks above the bridge, quacking loudly as they left the stream and waddled to the yard, and when Tarka came to where they had been, he left the water and ran after them. They beat their wings as they tried to fly from him, but he reached the file and scattered them, running through them and disappearing. Nearer and nearer came Deadlock, with Captain and Waterwitch leading the pack. Huntsman, whippers-in, and field were left behind, struggling through hedges and over banks.

Hounds were bewildered when they reached the yard. They ran with noses to ground in puzzled excitement. Captain's shrill voice told that Tarka had gone under a gate. Waterwitch followed the wet seals in the dust, but turned off along a track of larger webs. The line was tangled again. Deadlock threw his belving tongue. Other hounds followed, but the scent led only to a duck that beat its wings and quacked in terror before them. A man with a rake drove them off, shouting and threatening to strike them. Dewcrop spoke across the yard and the hounds galloped to her, but the line led to a gate which they tried to leap, hurling themselves up and falling from the top bar. A duck had gone under the gate, but not Tarka.

All scent was gone. Hounds rolled in the dust or trotted up to men and women, sniffing their pockets for food. Rufus found a rabbit skin and ate it; Render fought with Sandboy – but not seriously, as they feared each other; Deadlock went off alone. And hounds were

waiting for a lead
when the sweating
huntsman, grey pot-hat
pushed back from his red brow,
ran up with the two whippers-in
and called them into a pack again.
The thick scent of the Muscovy
ducks had checked the hunt.
Tarka had run through a drain back
to the stream, and now he rested in
the water that carried him every
moment nearer to the murmurous glooms of the glen
below. He saw the coloured blur of a kingfisher perch-
ing on a twig as it eyes the water for beetle or loach. The
kingfisher saw him moving under the surface, as his
shadow broke the net of ripple shadows that drifted in
meshes of pale gold on the stony bed beneath him.

While he was walking past the roots of a willow under
the bank, he heard the yapping of the terrier. Sammy

had crept through the drain, and was looking out at the end, covered with black filth, and eagerly telling his big friends to follow him downstream. As he yapped, Deadlock threw his tongue. The stallion hound was below the drain, and had re-found the line where Tarka had last touched the shillets. Tarka saw him, ten yards away, and slipping back into the water, swam with all webs down the current, pushing from his nose a ream whose shadow beneath was an arrow of gold pointing down to the sea.

Again he quitted the water and ran on land to wear away his scent. He had gone twenty yards when Deadlock scrambled up the bank with Render and Sandboy, breathing the scent which was as high as their muzzles. Tarka reached the waterside trees again a length ahead of Deadlock, and fell into the water like a sodden log. Deadlock leapt after him and snapped at his head; but the water was friendly to the otter, who rolled in smooth and graceful movement away from the jaws, a straight bite of which would have crushed his skull.

Here sunlight was shut out by the oaks, and the roar of the first fall was beating back from the leaves. The current ran faster, narrowing into a race with twirls and hollows marking the sunken rocks. The roar grew louder in a drifting spray. Tarka and Deadlock were carried to where a broad sunbeam came down through a break in the foliage and lit the mist above the fall. Tarka went over the heavy white folds of the torrent and Deadlock was hurled over after him. They were lost in the churn and pressure of the pool until a small brown head appeared and gazed for its enemy in the broken honeycomb of foam. A black and white body uprolled beside it, and the head of the hound was thrust up as he tried to tread away from the current that would draw him under. Tarka was master of whirlpools; they were his playthings. He rocked in the surge with delight; then high above he heard the note of the horn. He yielded himself to the water and let it take him away down the gorge into a pool where rocks were piled above. He searched under the dripping ferny clitter for a hiding-place.

Under water he saw two legs, joined to two wavering and inverted images of legs, and above the blurred shapes of a man's head and shoulders. He turned away from the fisherman into the current again and as he breathed he heard the horn again. On the road above the glen the pack was trotting between huntsman and whippers-in, and before them men were running with poles at the trail, hurrying down the hill to the bridge, to make a stickle to stop Tarka reaching the sea.

Tarka left Deadlock far behind. The hound was feeble and bruised and breathing harshly, his head battered and his sight dazed, but still following. Tarka passed another fisherman, and by chance the tiny feathered hook lodged in his ear. The reel spun against the check, *re-re-re* continuously, until all the silken line had run through the snake-rings of the rod, which bent into a circle, and whipped back straight again as the gut trace snapped.

Tarka saw the bridge, the figure of a man below it, and a row of faces above. He heard shouts. The man standing on a rock took off his hat, scooped the air, and holla'd to the huntsman, who was running and slipping with the pack on the loose stones of the steep red road. Tarka walked out of the last pool above the bridge, ran over a mossy rock, merged with the water again, and pushed through the legs of the man.

Tally-ho!

Tarka had gone under the bridge when Harper splashed into the water. The pack poured through the gap between the end of the parapet and the hillside earth, and their tongues rang under the bridge and down the walls of the houses built on the rock above the river.

Among rotting motor tyres, broken bottles, tins, pails, shoes, and other castaway rubbish lying in the bright water, hounds made their plunging leaps. Once Tarka turned back; often he was splashed and trodden on. The stream was seldom deep enough to cover him, and always shallow enough for the hounds to move at double his speed. Sometimes he was under the pack, and then, while hounds were massing for the worry, his small head would look out beside a rock ten yards below them.

Between boulders and rocks crusted with shellfish and shaggy with seaweed, past worm-channered posts that marked the fairway for fishing boats at high water, the pack hunted the otter. Off each post a gull launched itself, cackling angrily as it looked down at the animals. Tarka reached the sea. He walked slowly into the surge of a wavelet, and sank away from the chop of old Harper's jaws, just as Deadlock ran through the pack. Hounds swam beyond the line of waves, while people stood at the sealap and watched the huntsman wading to his waist. It was said that the otter was dead-beat, and probably floating stiffly in the shallow-water. After a few minutes the huntsman shook his head, and withdrew the horn from his waistcoat. He filled his lungs and stopped his breath and was tightening his lips for the four long notes of the call-off, when a brown head with hard dark eyes was thrust out of the water a yard from Deadlock. Tarka stared into the hound's face and cried *Ic-yang!*

The head sank. Swimming under Deadlock, Tarka bit on to the loose skin of the flews and pulled the hound's head under water. Deadlock tried to twist round and crush the otter's skull in his jaws, but he struggled vainly. Bubbles blew out of his mouth. Soon he was choking. The hounds did not know what was happening. Deadlock's hind-legs kicked the air weakly. The huntsman waded out and pulled him inshore, but Tarka loosened his bite only when he needed new air in his lungs; and then he swam under and gripped Deadlock again. Only when hounds were upon him did Tarka let go. He vanished in a wave.

Long after the water had been emptied out of Deadlock's lungs, and the pack had trotted off for the long uphill climb to the railway station, the gulls were flying over something in the sea beyond the mouth of the little estuary. Sometimes one dropped its yellow webs to alight on the water; always it flew up again into the restless, wailing throng, startled by the snaps of white teeth. A cargo steamer was passing up the Severn Sea, leaving a long smudge of smoke on the horizon, where a low line of clouds billowed over the coast of Wales. The regular thumps of its screw in the windless blue calm were borne to where Tarka lay, drowsy and content, but watching the pale yellow eyes of the nearest bird. At last the gulls grew tired of seeing only his eyes, and flew back to their posts; and turning on his back, Tarka yawned and stretched himself, and floated at his ease.

Glossary of
Difficult Words

The Ugly Duckling
syringa – a blue-flowered tree with long hanging branches

The Jungle
crème d'amande pour la barbe et les mains – almond cream for shaving and for the hands
malacca – bamboo, a form of wood found in hot countries

Lassie Comes Over the Border
incandescent – light coming from heat

Black Beauty
purblind – half-blind

Roy
nostrums – home-made medicines
necrotic tissue – dead skin and flesh
granulating – in this case it means that the wounds were drying out and hardening
noisome – evil-smelling

How the Leopard got his Spots
'sclusively – shortened form of exclusively which means belonging to one group or individual
fulvous – sandy-brown

The Cat that Walked by Himself

fenugreek – a heavily scented plant

grenadilla – a bush which has fruit

An Otter Hunt

shillets – shale, a type of rock

law – to get a head start

bine – a stem of a climbing plant

insinuated – slithered

runnel – a small stream

plash – a hedge

belving – catching the scent with the tongue

loach – a freshwater fish

clitter – a tangled mass, jumble

stickle – to argue or refuse to agree

worm-channered – worm-eaten

flews – upper lips of a hound

Illustration Credits

6, 29, 73, 84, 123, 185, © 1989 by Robert Cook; 97, 98 by W.W. Denslow; 176, 178 © by Janet and Anne Graham-Johnstone; 21, 24, 26 © by W. Heath Robinson; 103, 111 by Lucy Kemp-Welch from a limited edition, courtesy Susan Miles; 137, 143 by Rudyard Kipling; 55, 57 by John Nicolson; 34, 35, 37, 40 by James Short.

Acknowledgements

The Publisher has made every effort to contact the Copyright holders, but wishes to apologise to those he has been unable to trace. Grateful acknowledgement is made for permission to reprint the following:

Prince Rabbit by A.A. Milne. Copyright A.A. Milne 1924, reproduced by permission of Curtis Brown Ltd, London.

'Lassie Comes Over the Border' from *Lassie Come Home* by Eric Knight. By permission of Cassell PLC (UK) and Curtis Brown Ltd, New York (US). Copyright © 1940 by Jere Knight. Copyright renewed 1968 by Jere Knight, Betty Noyes Knight, Winifred Knight Newborn, and Jenny Knight Moore.

'Roy' from *All Things Bright and Beautiful* by James Herriot. By permission of David Higham Associates Ltd (UK) and St Martin's Press, Inc., New York (US). Copyright © 1973, 1974 by James Herriot.

'The Boy Who Talked With Animals' from *The Wonderful Story of Henry Sugar* by Roald Dahl (courtesy Jonathan Cape Ltd and Penguin Books Ltd), reproduced by permission of Murray Pollinger (UK) and Alfred A. Knopf, Inc., (US). Copyright 1945, 1947, 1952, © 1977 by Roald Dahl. (*The Wonderful World of Henry Sugar and Six More* by Roald Dahl.)

'Christmas Eve' from *The Hundred and One Dalmatians* by Dodie Smith. Reprinted by permission of William Heinemann Ltd (UK) and Viking Penguin Inc., New York (US). Copyright © 1956, renewed © 1984 by Dodie Smith. Reprinted by permission of Viking Penguin, a division of Penguin Books USA, Inc. Illustrations courtesy Janet and Anne Graham-Johnstone.

'An Otter Hunt' from *Tarka the Otter* by Henry Williamson. Courtesy the Estate of Henry Williamson.

$$\begin{array}{r} 0\,7\,7\tfrac{1}{2} \\ 2\overline{)1\,5\,5} \end{array}$$

$$\begin{array}{r} 0\,8\,6 \\ 2\overline{)1\,7\,2} \end{array}$$